To the Blitch Family!
With love!
R

This book is dedicated to all who love Afghanistan, the beauty of her people, rugged topography, rich history, antiquities, architecture, cultural diversity, indigenous animals, precious resources, delicious food, snow-capped mountains, and fertile valleys. And to my Afghan friends, Esmatullah and Jaweed, both of whom I first met in 2004 and again, in 2008, who forever enriched my life with their dignity, authenticity, and open hearts. Finally, I offer this book to my family and friends for unyielding support and the gifts of inspiration through opportunities.

How the Ariana Crickets Got Their Chirp Back

Published by Clovercroft Publishing, Franklin, Tennessee

Illustrated by Sally Kat

Cover and Interior Design by Suzanne Lawing

ISBN: 978-1-945507-86-1

Printed in the United States of America

Lovie R. Smith

Illustrated by Sally Kat

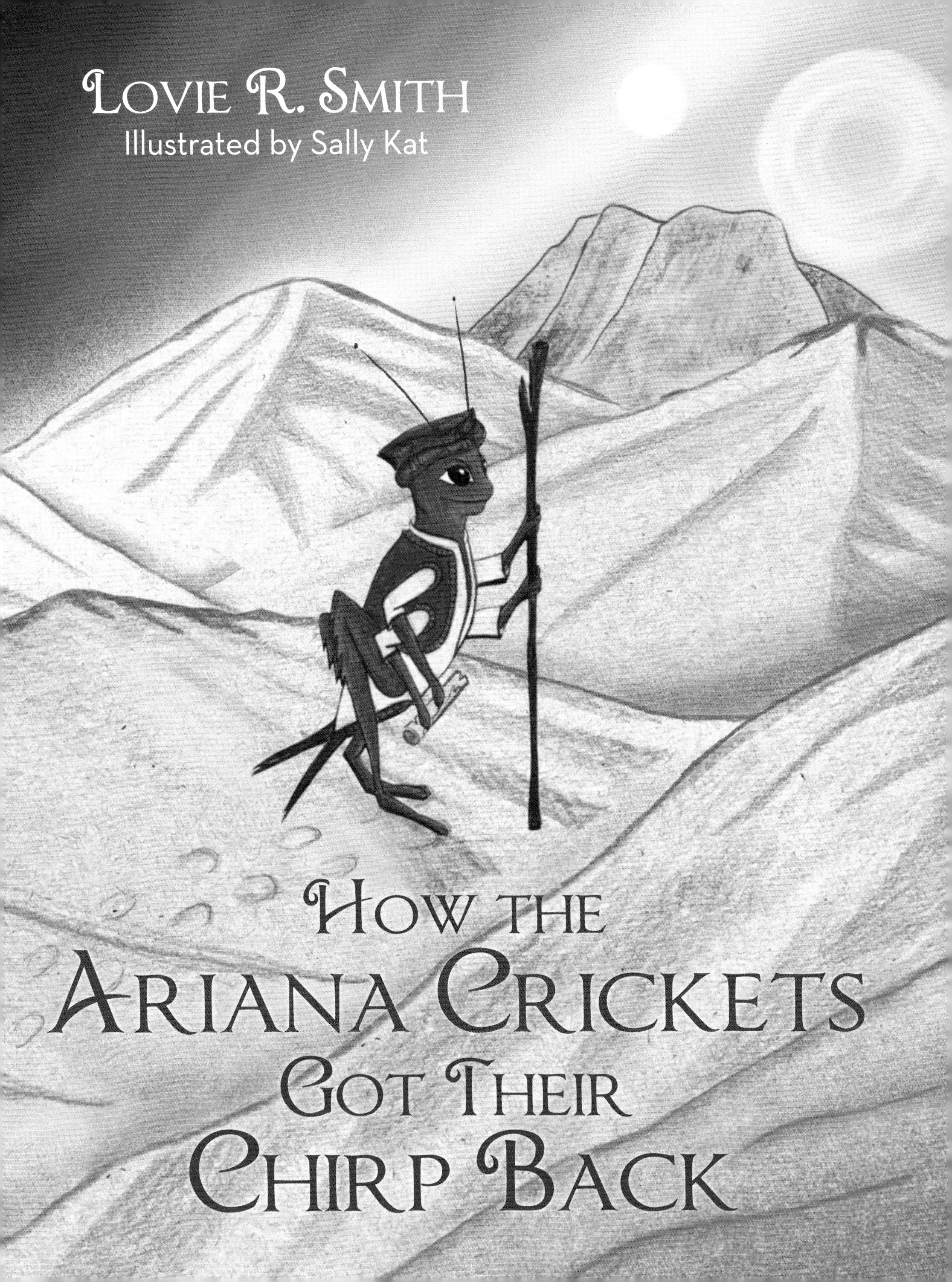

How the Ariana Crickets Got Their Chirp Back

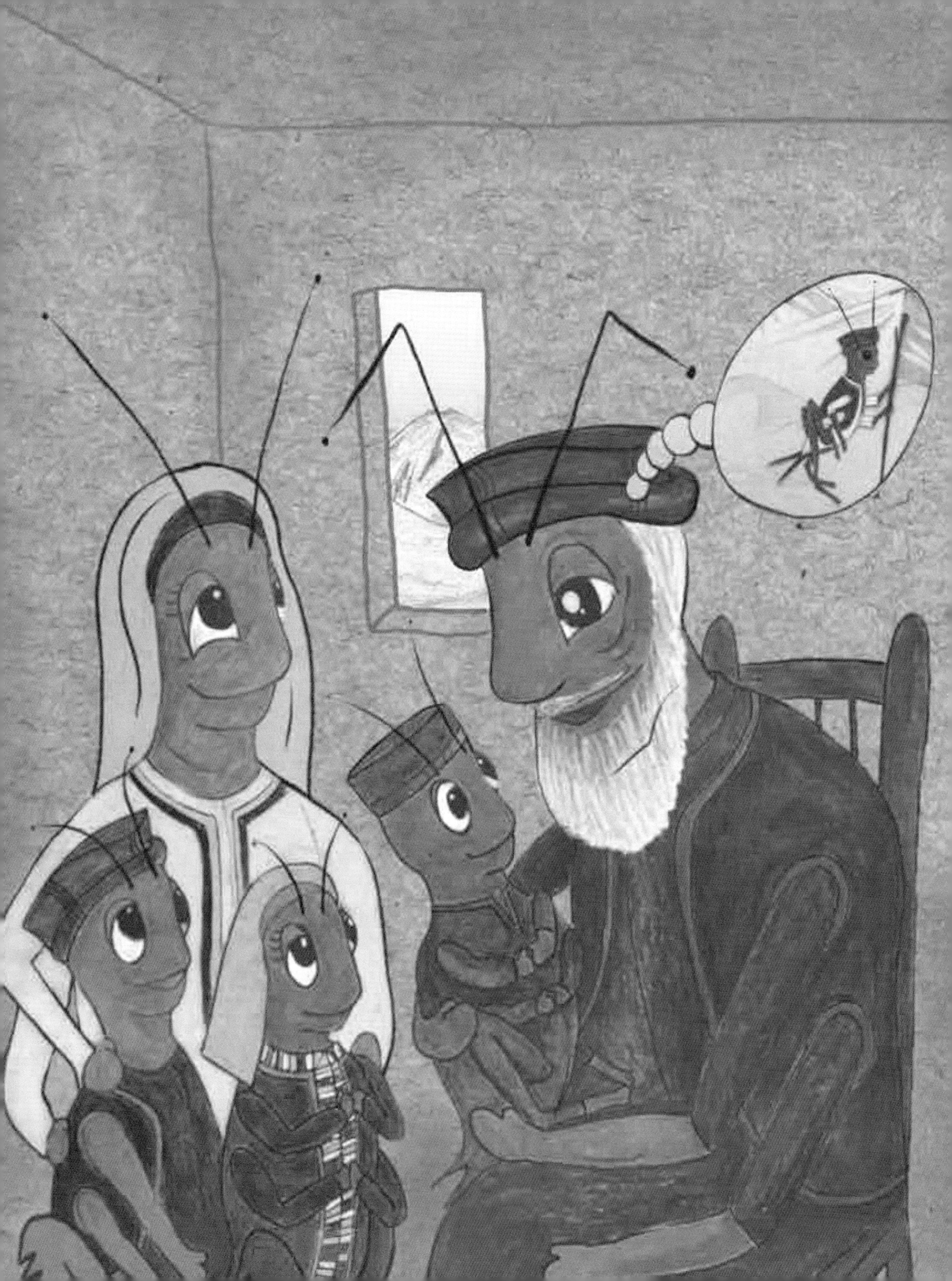

"Grandfather Ahmad, one more time! Tell us how the Ariana crickets got their chirp back!" the grandchildren asked. I smiled and dreamed. I'm an old cricket now. But, I remember. I remember everything. With the youngest grandchild sitting on my lap, I began my story.

One day, a long time ago, the sky stopped raining. The rain stayed away for forever. The ground was dry, leaves curled upside down and fell to the ground, birds stopped singing and, well, we stopped having fun. Everyone was quiet and whispered all the time. Cricket families stayed inside. We didn't fly kites or sing or dance. There was absolutely no chirping. No crickets chirping? Preposterous! Absurd!

Crickets all over Ariana had just stopped chirping. We hadn't chirped in so long, most had forgotten how. Every living thing longed to hear the chirp, chirp songs of crickets.

Legend had it that crickets chirping everywhere, all together at the same time, was the only way to make it rain again. And, rain would bring healing. This miracle could only happen when nighttime falls during the day!

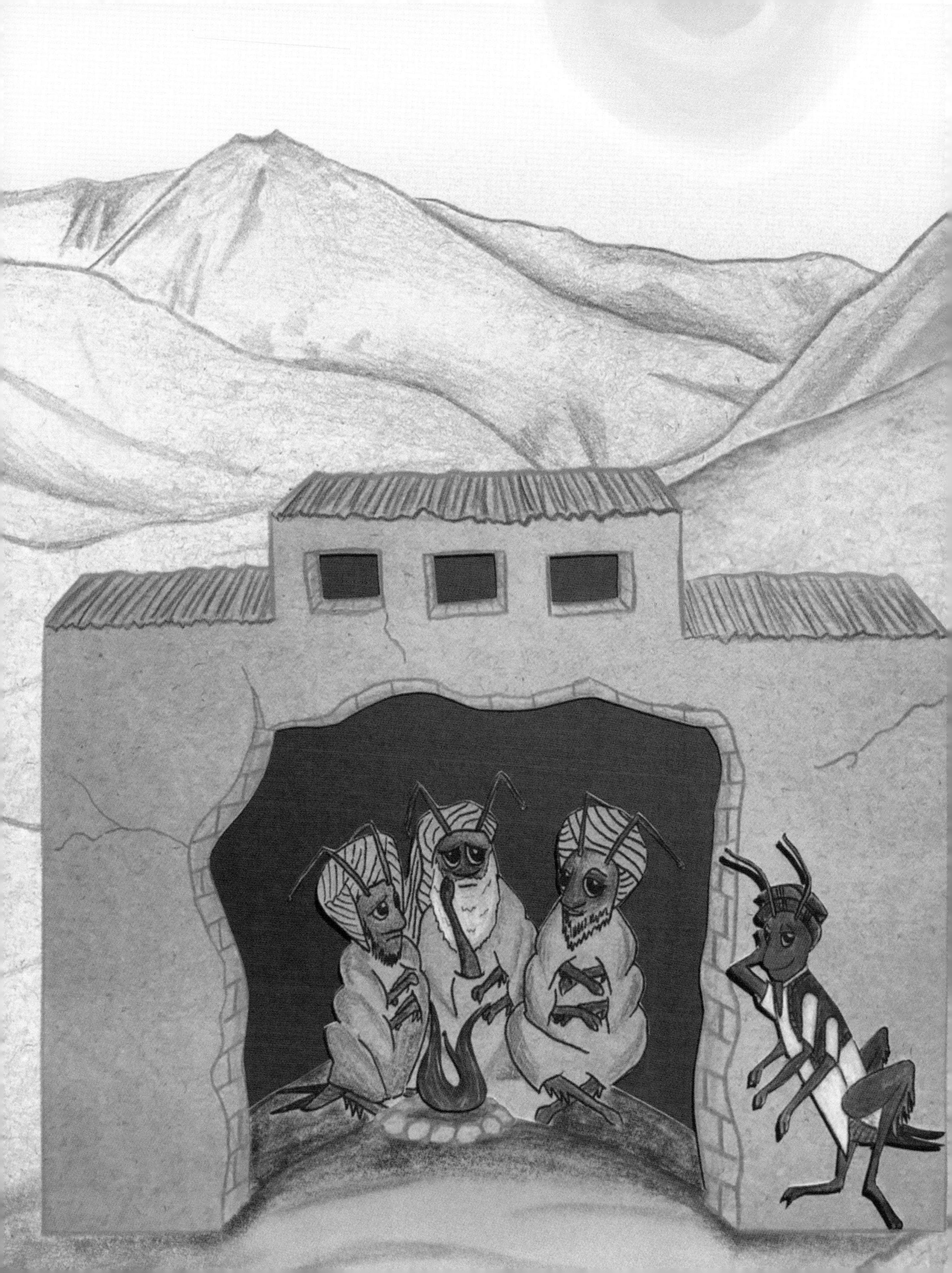

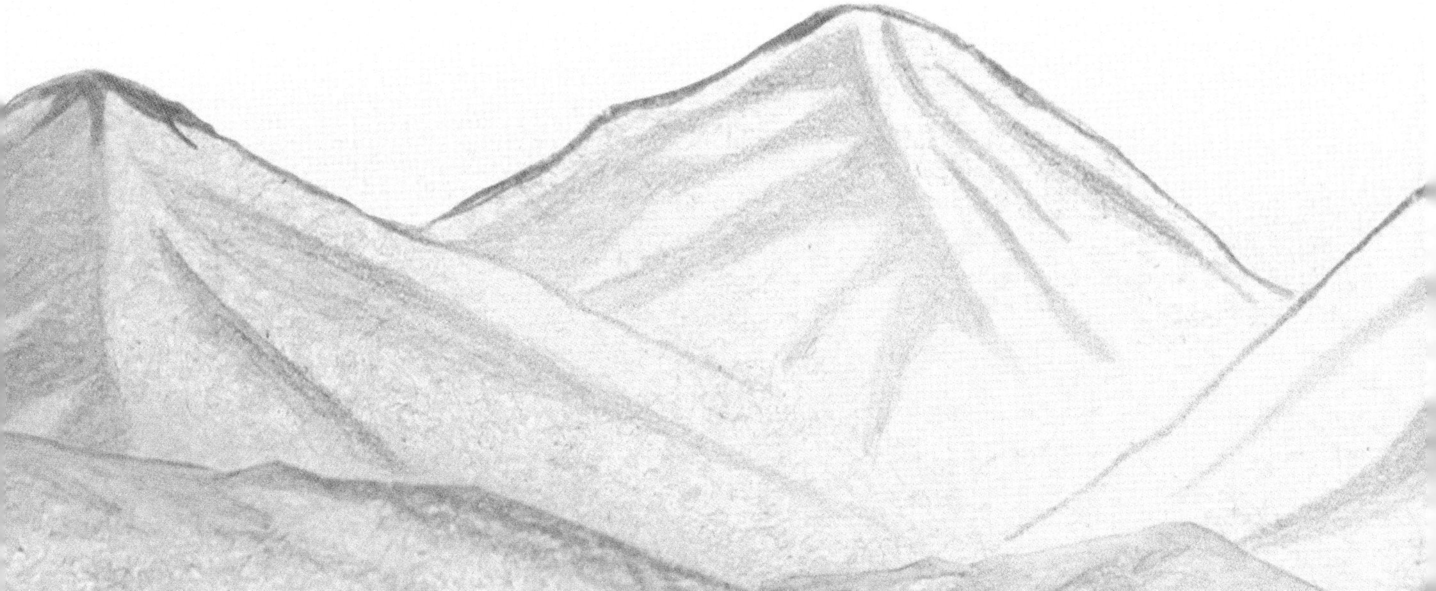

I was a just a young cricket then. Growing up fast, I wanted to run and jump, fly kites, and chirp day and night. Make a difference! Do something important. More than anything, I wanted to chirp. One day, I overheard my Grandfather, Uncle, and Father inside the hut.

"Rain.. . .teach. . ..chirp." I was only able to hear some of what they said. "Get. . ..chirps.. . .back," Esmatullah, my Father whispered. Uncle Nasrat said, "The time for healing is near. We must work fast!"

"What. . ..?" My curiosity was piqued. I listened further.

Esmatullah went on, "The moon will pass in front of the sun, causing the night to come during the day. Cricket clans must learn to chirp before that day to heal the land. Crickets who've never chirped will jump high and raise their wings to the sky when the sun hides behind the moon. One of us must teach all crickets to chirp before that day."

This sounded like my chance to do something big! I listened further and peeked in the door.

"Which one of us?" asked Uncle Nasrat.

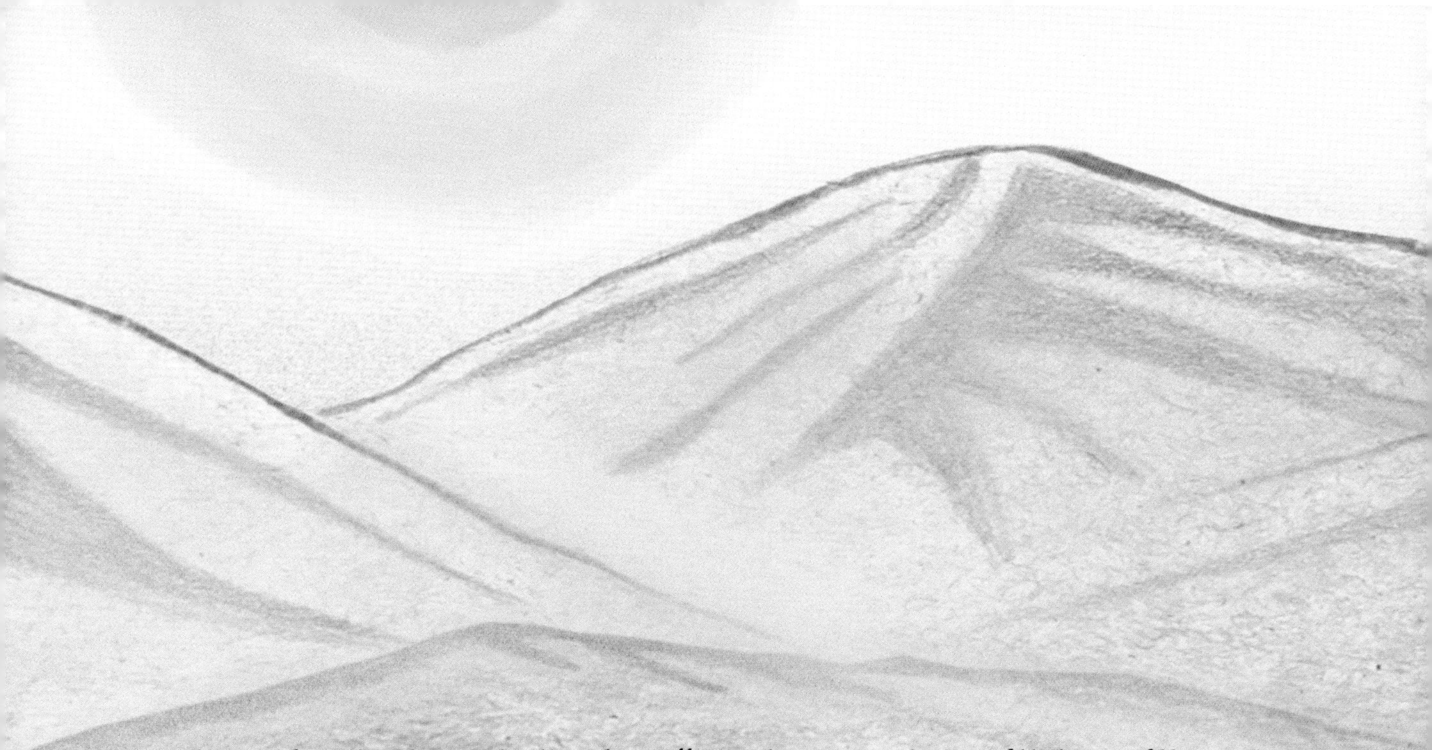

I hopped right through that door. "Teach me to chirp. I'll do it. I'll teach every cricket across the land to chirp again. Then, the rain will fall again."

Grandfather was quiet for a long time. "Ahmad, you're brave and strong. And, you help others." "He's friendly, too!" the others chittered.

Those grizzled crickets recalled about a time long ago when music, laughing and chirps were heard everywhere. Golden wheat fields grew to the sky. Grapes were fat, full, and fell to the ground with a thunk. Kites flew to the other side of the clouds. Swings swung high, almost to the sky! Rain had smelled so sweet.

"It's settled. Teach me to chirp—long chirps, short ones, fast and slow, quiet chirps and loud chirps! Morning and night songs. I'll teach our crickets to chirp. Then, we can sing and dance, fly kites, swing high to the sky, play music, and chirp as loud as loud can be! I AM the cricket for this job! And, I'll tell my children how the Ariana crickets got their chirp back!"

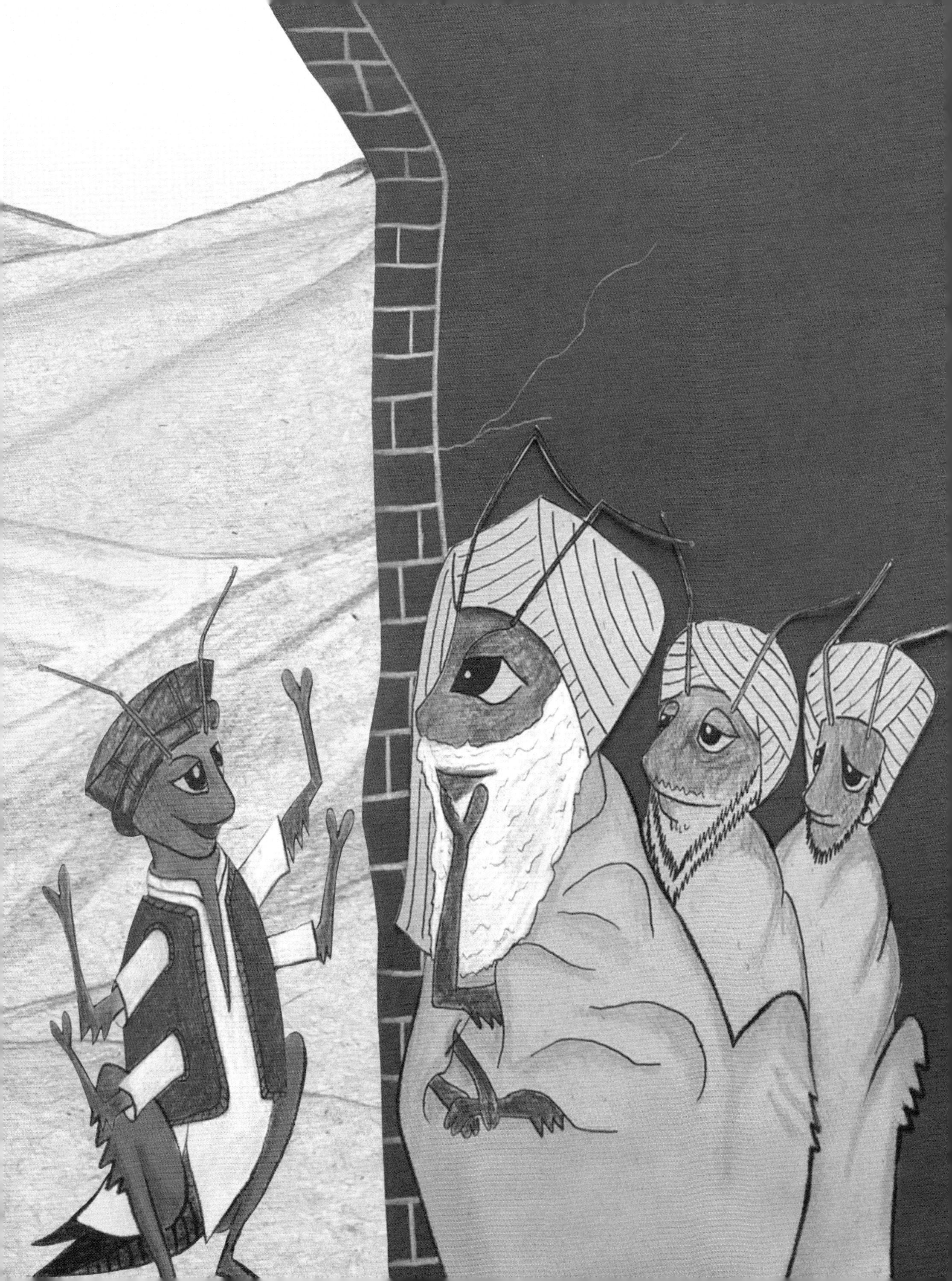

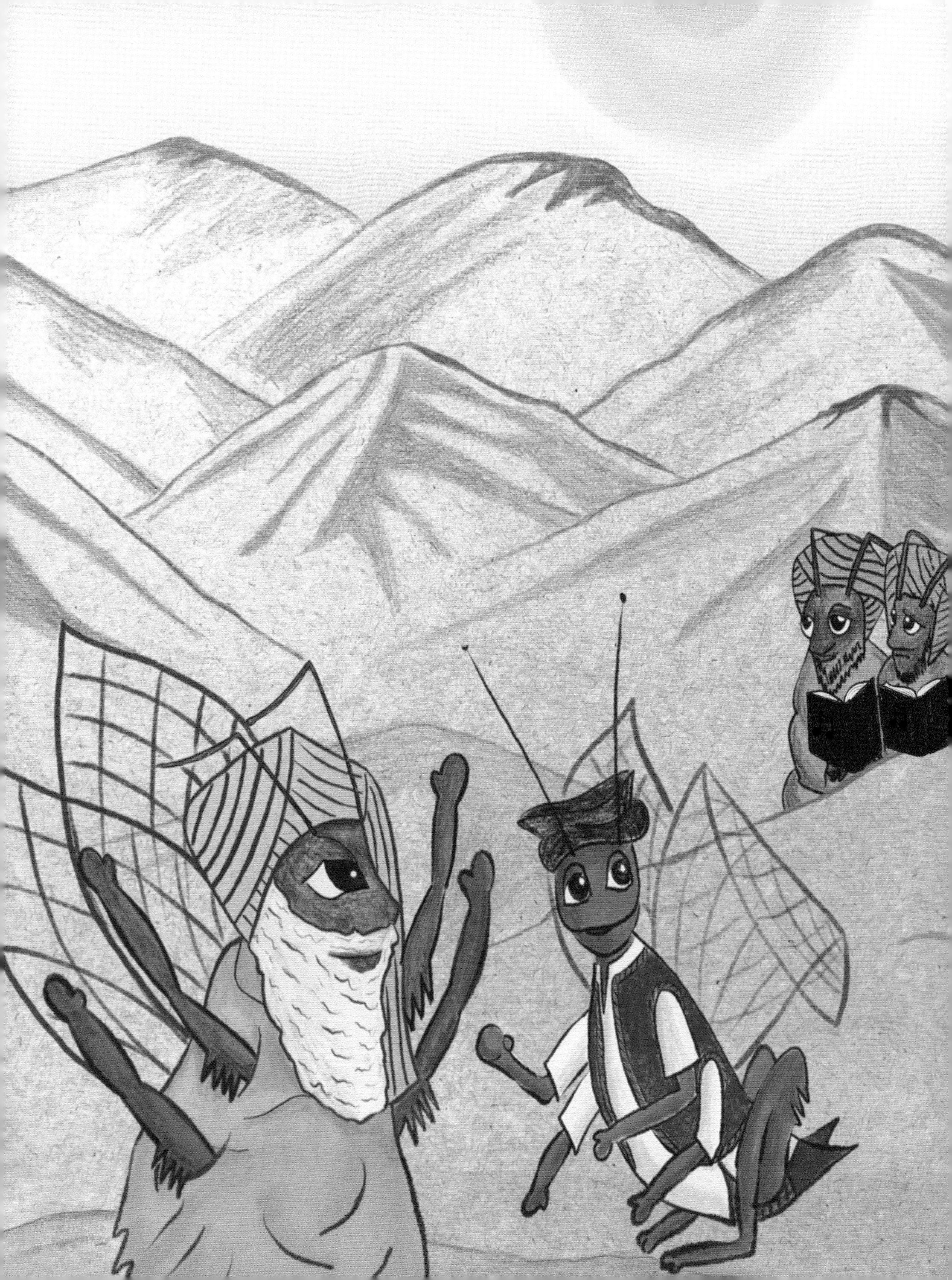

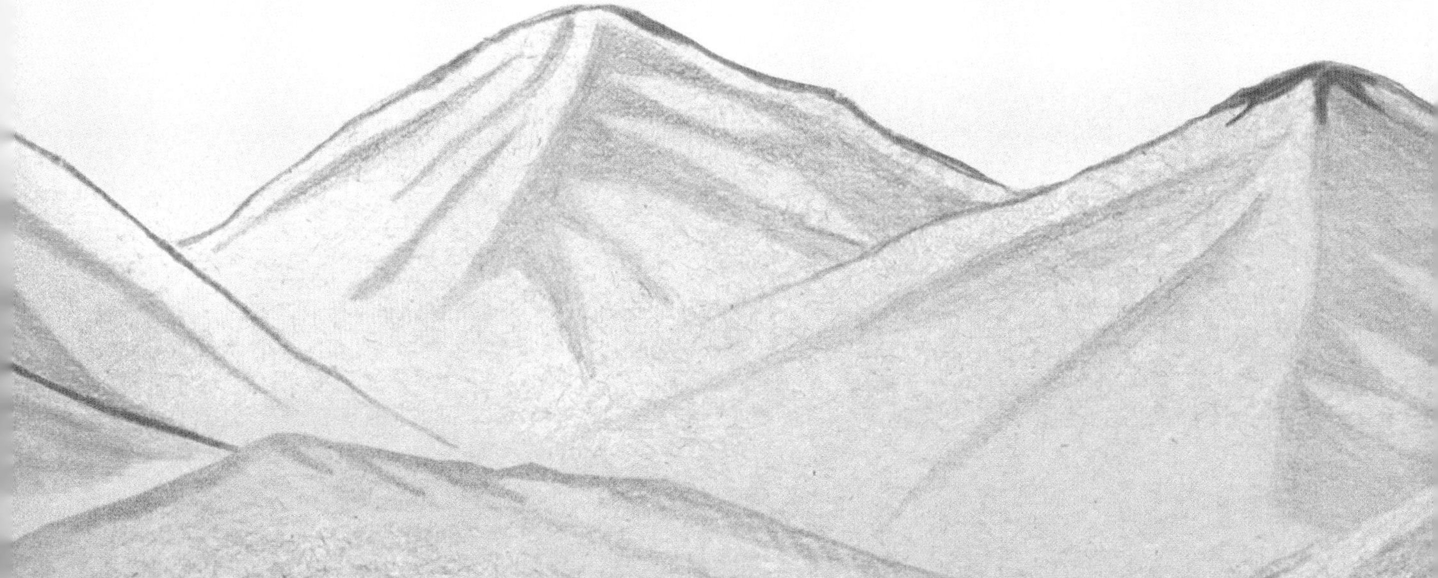

Later that afternoon, with old songbooks in hand, my chirp lessons started. At first, I lifted and flapped my wings but no sounds came out! "Ahmad, watch and listen," fussed Esmatullah.

Nasrat asked me to focus, "Look closely at your left wing. See the ridges there? Those ridges are like strings on a sarangi. Now, lift your right wing. The top of your right wing is a scraper—like a bow that you press and move along sarangi strings. Next, and at the same time, raise and turn your left wing and brush your right wing against the ridges. That's it! That's the chirping sound. The technical name for the sound is stridulation. We just call it chirping, because that's a lot easier to say."

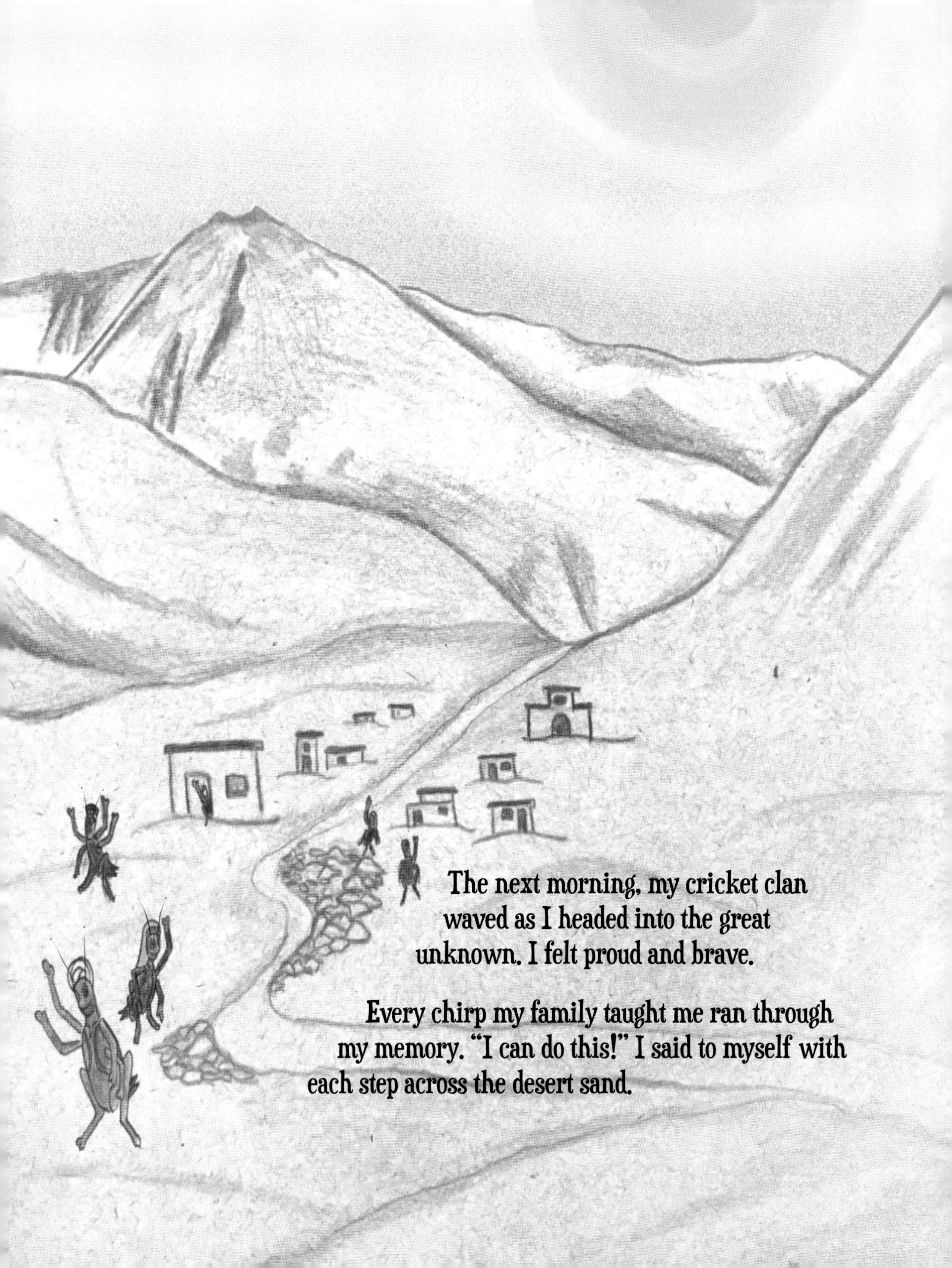

The next morning, my cricket clan waved as I headed into the great unknown. I felt proud and brave.

Every chirp my family taught me ran through my memory. "I can do this!" I said to myself with each step across the desert sand.

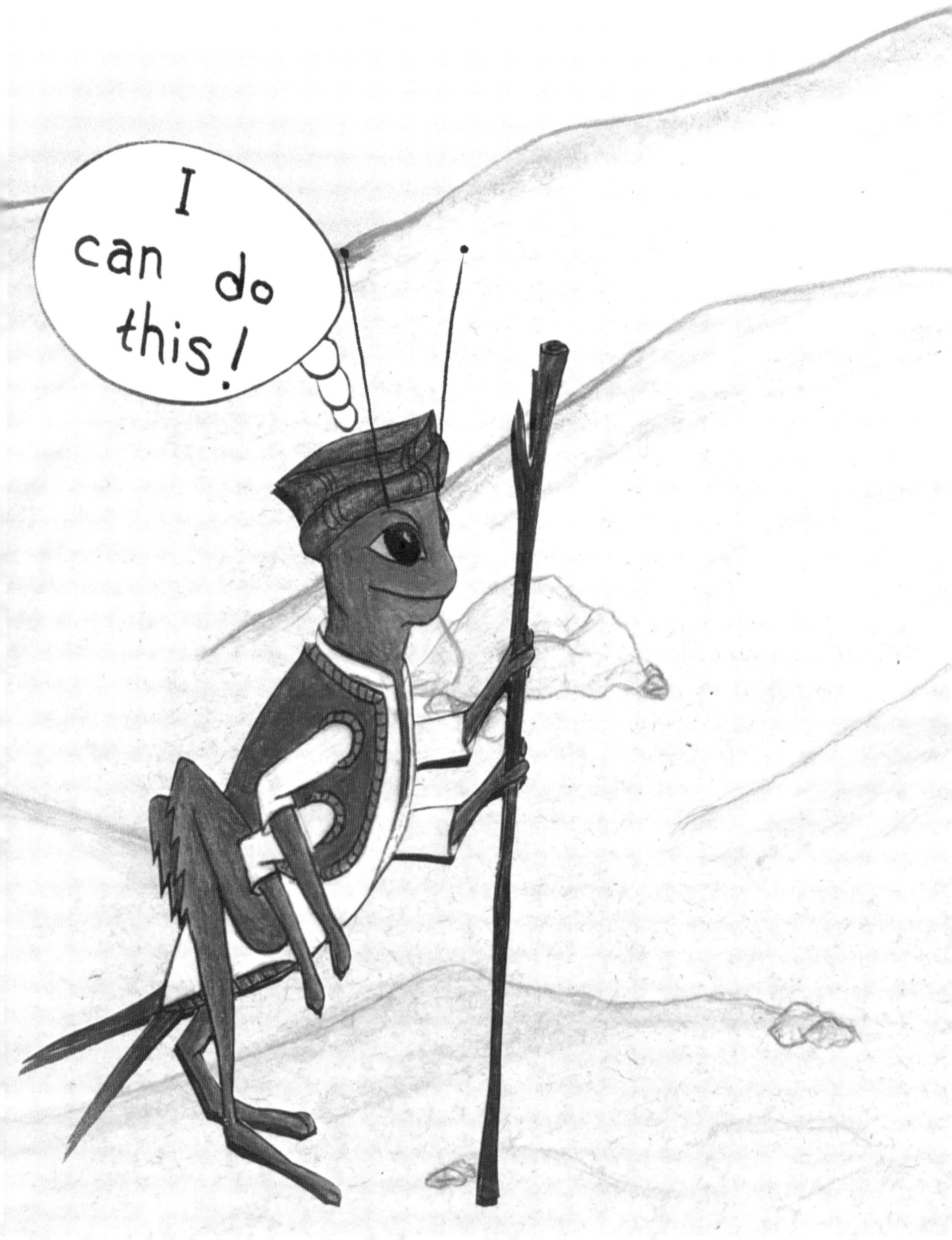
I can do this!

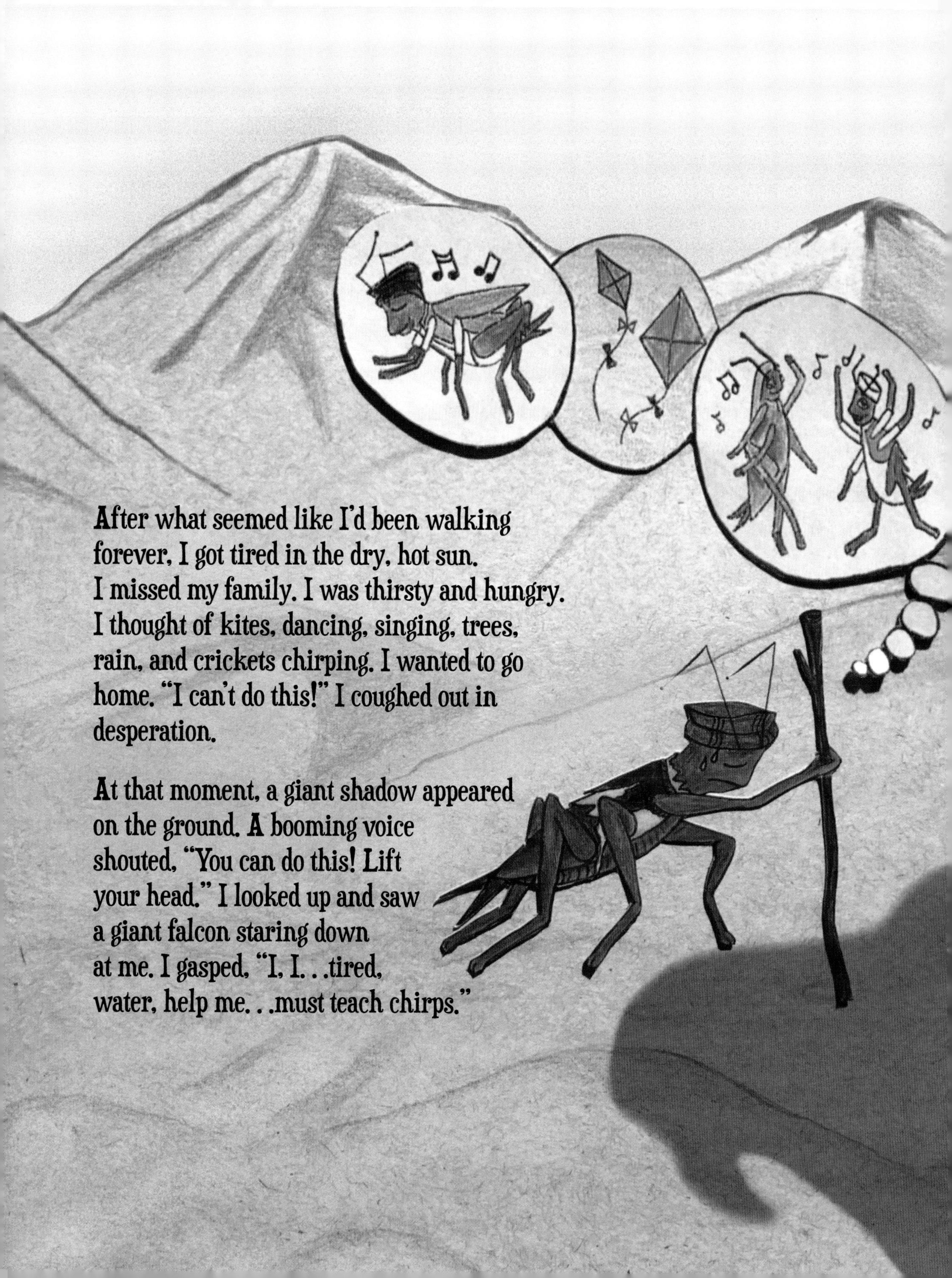

After what seemed like I'd been walking forever, I got tired in the dry, hot sun. I missed my family. I was thirsty and hungry. I thought of kites, dancing, singing, trees, rain, and crickets chirping. I wanted to go home. "I can't do this!" I coughed out in desperation.

At that moment, a giant shadow appeared on the ground. A booming voice shouted, "You can do this! Lift your head." I looked up and saw a giant falcon staring down at me. I gasped, "I, I. . .tired, water, help me. . .must teach chirps."

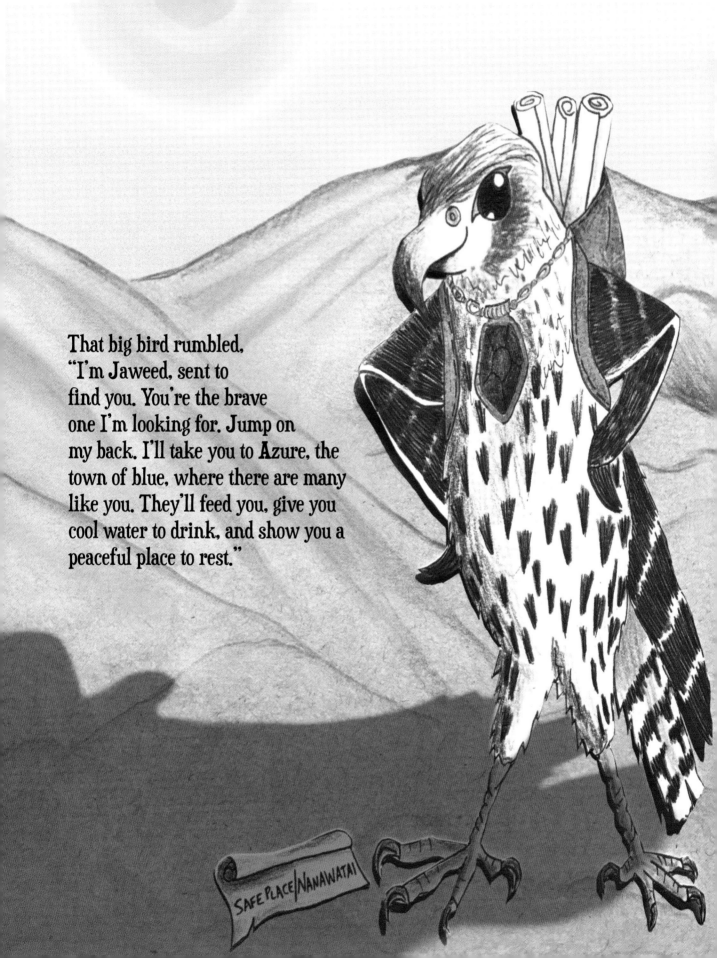

That big bird rumbled, "I'm Jaweed, sent to find you. You're the brave one I'm looking for. Jump on my back. I'll take you to **Azure**, the town of blue, where there are many like you. They'll feed you, give you cool water to drink, and show you a peaceful place to rest."

SAFE PLACE/NANAWATAI

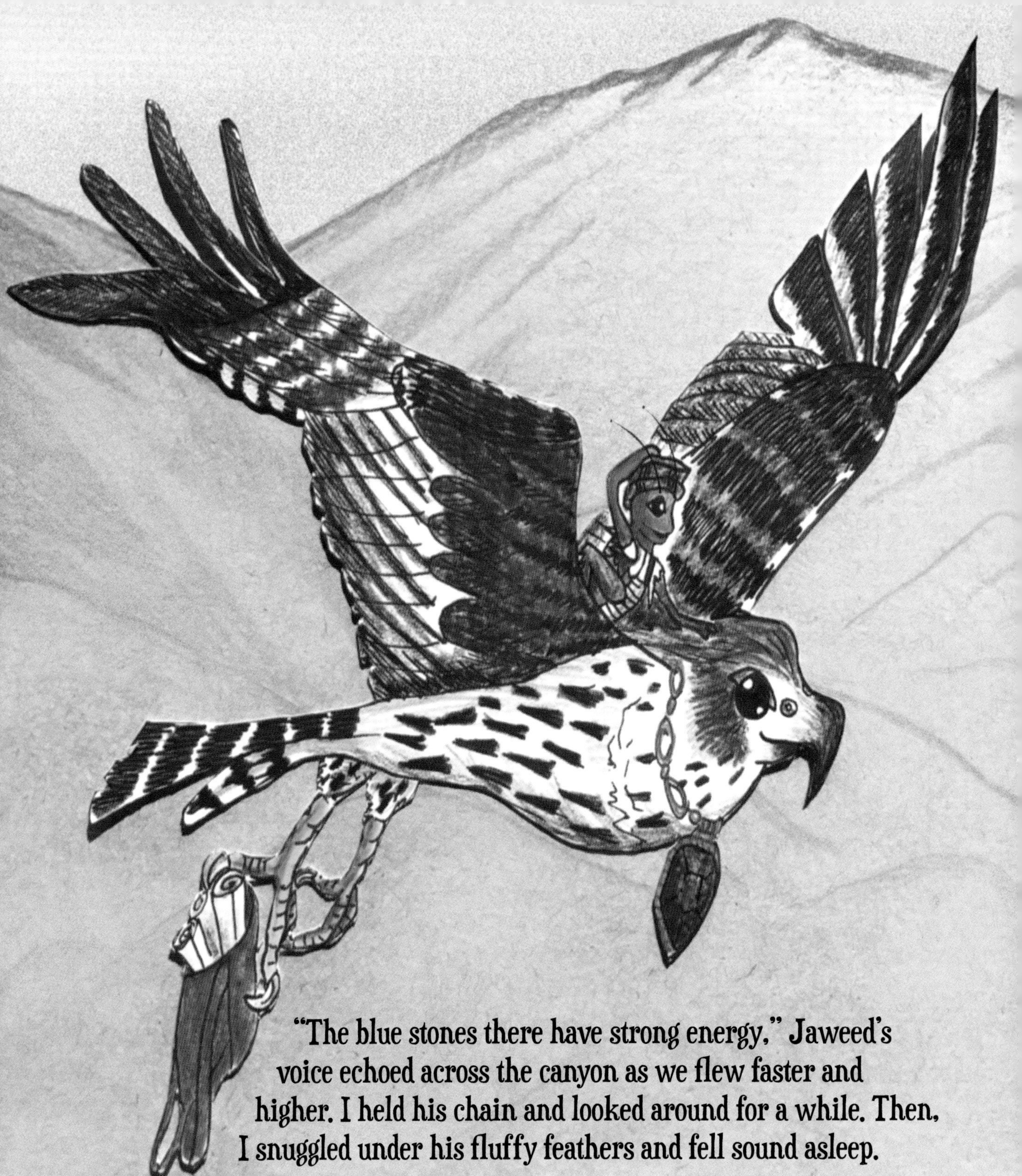

"The blue stones there have strong energy," Jaweed's voice echoed across the canyon as we flew faster and higher. I held his chain and looked around for a while. Then, I snuggled under his fluffy feathers and fell sound asleep.

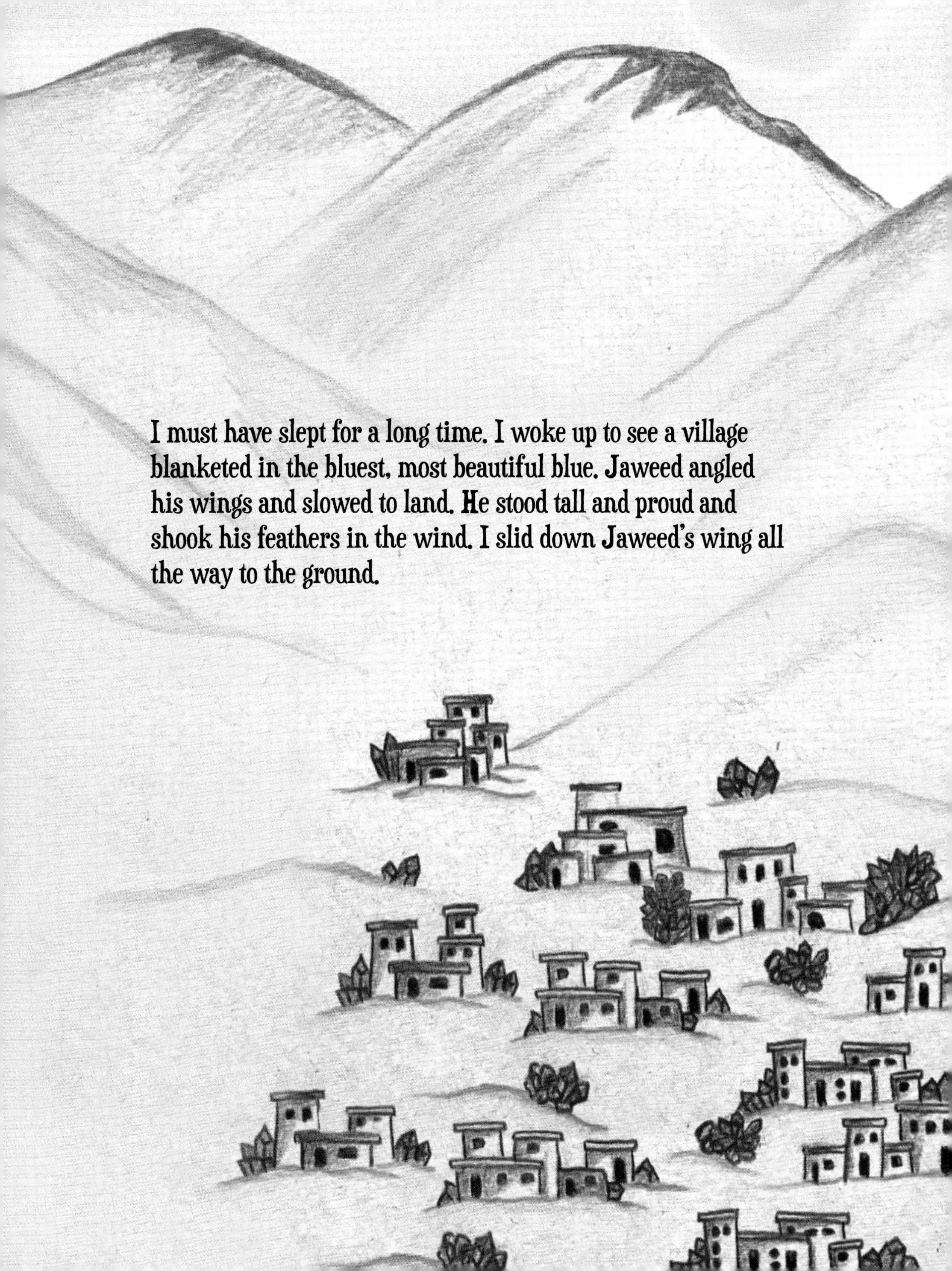

I must have slept for a long time. I woke up to see a village blanketed in the bluest, most beautiful blue. Jaweed angled his wings and slowed to land. He stood tall and proud and shook his feathers in the wind. I slid down Jaweed's wing all the way to the ground.

He led me to a warm cricket home and said, "Rest here, these blue stones will cheer you up." I sat in the middle of those stones for a long time. Soon, crickets were all around me. The crickets in that town were different from me, but we were mostly the same. We ate rice and onions. They gave me new clothes.

Suddenly, my strength came back. I hopped around the house. Then, I warbled out the loudest cricket chirp ever heard. My friends' eyes opened wide. Some hid their faces. Others jumped behind rugs. I chirped, "Do not fear! Watch me. Do what I do. You can try it, too!" Soon, the blue village crickets were chirping and hopping all around.

"One day soon," I chirped, "the sun will slide behind the moon. Before then, I'll teach crickets to chirp again. We'll chirp all at the same time as the sun takes a short nap. And, then it will rain. Grapes and figs will grow, and wheat will dance in the fields. We can sing, fly kites, and swing high again! We'll chirp all the time, every day, forever and ever!"

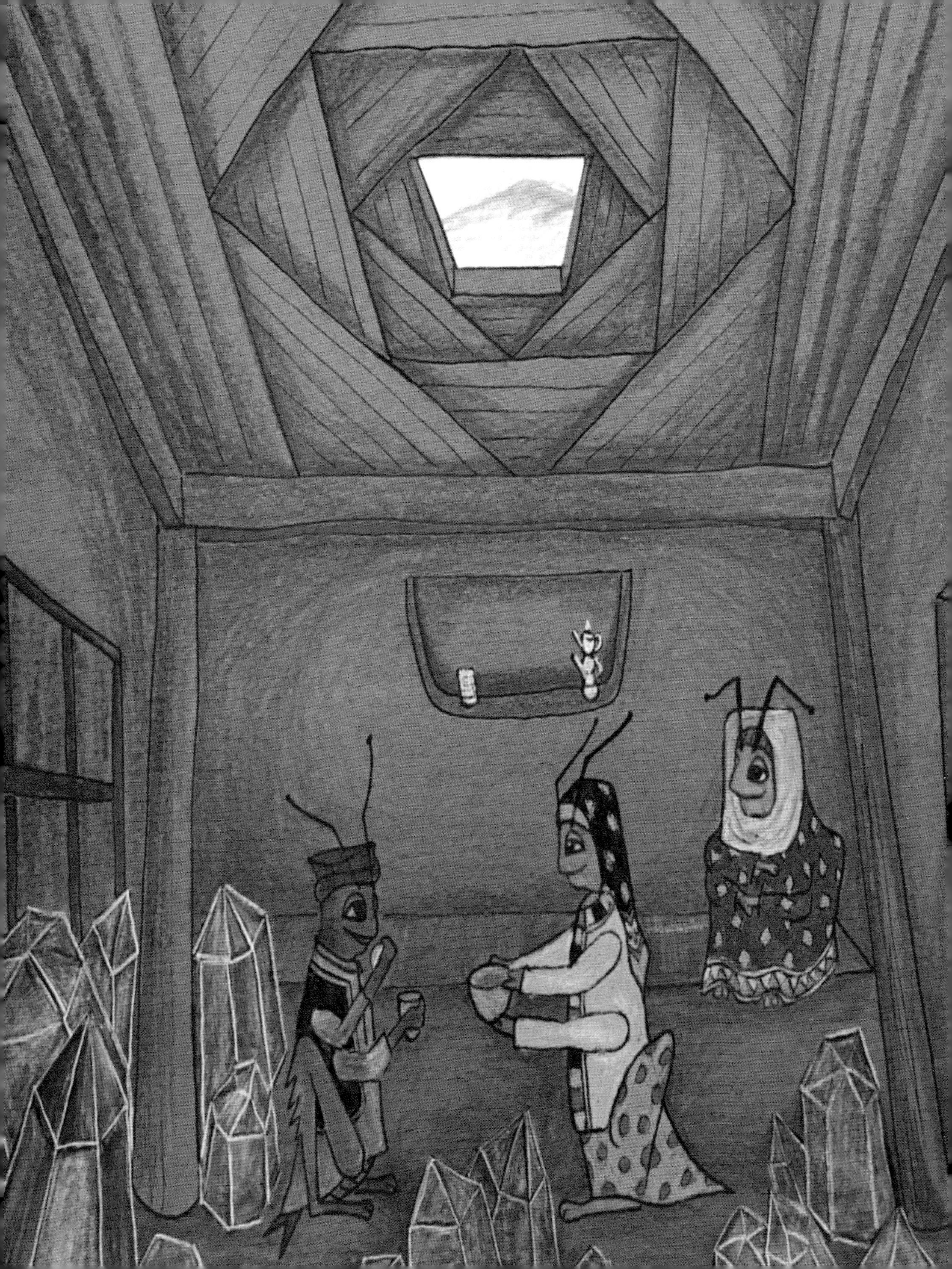

Those Azure crickets learned every chirp possible. Before the day was over, you could hear chirping sounds everywhere, just like a song that could go on and on, forever and ever, until the end of time. Just as the sun went down for the night, the bluest raindrops fell from the sky.

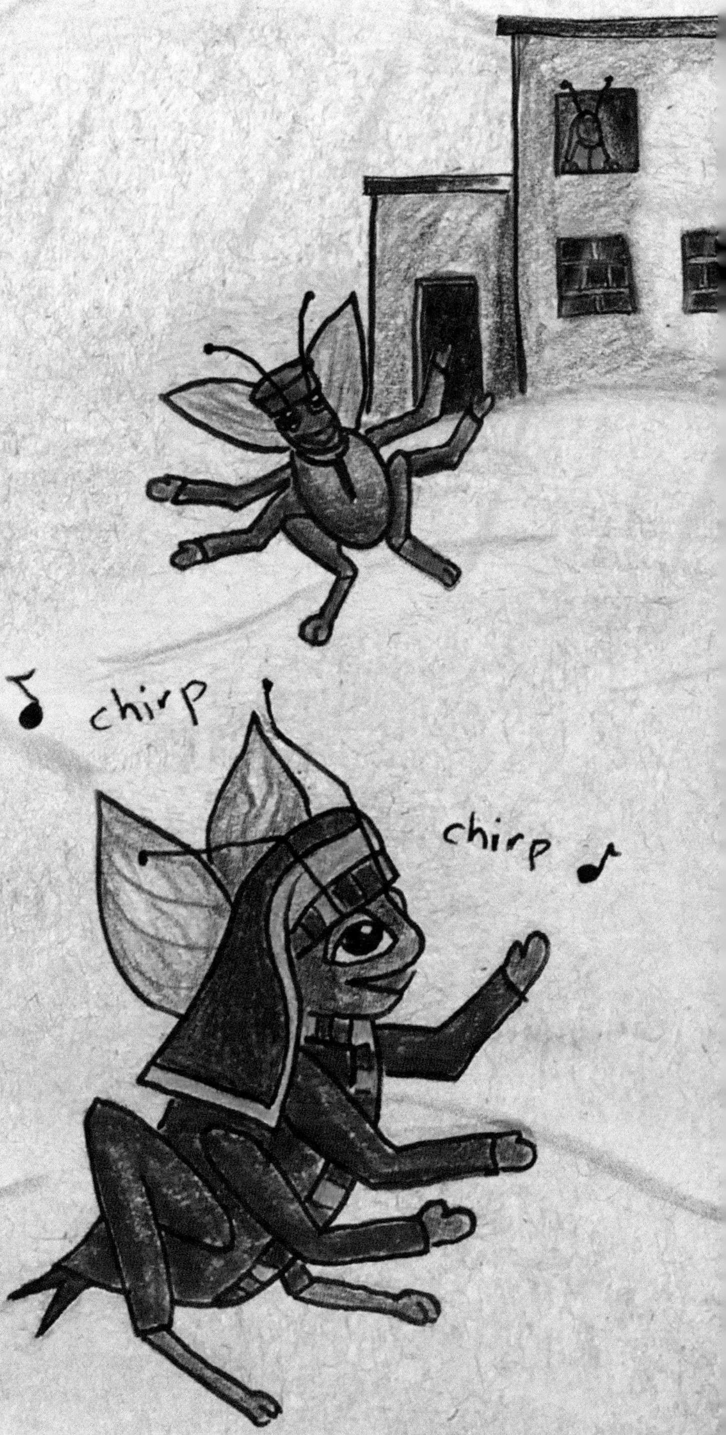
chirp
chirp

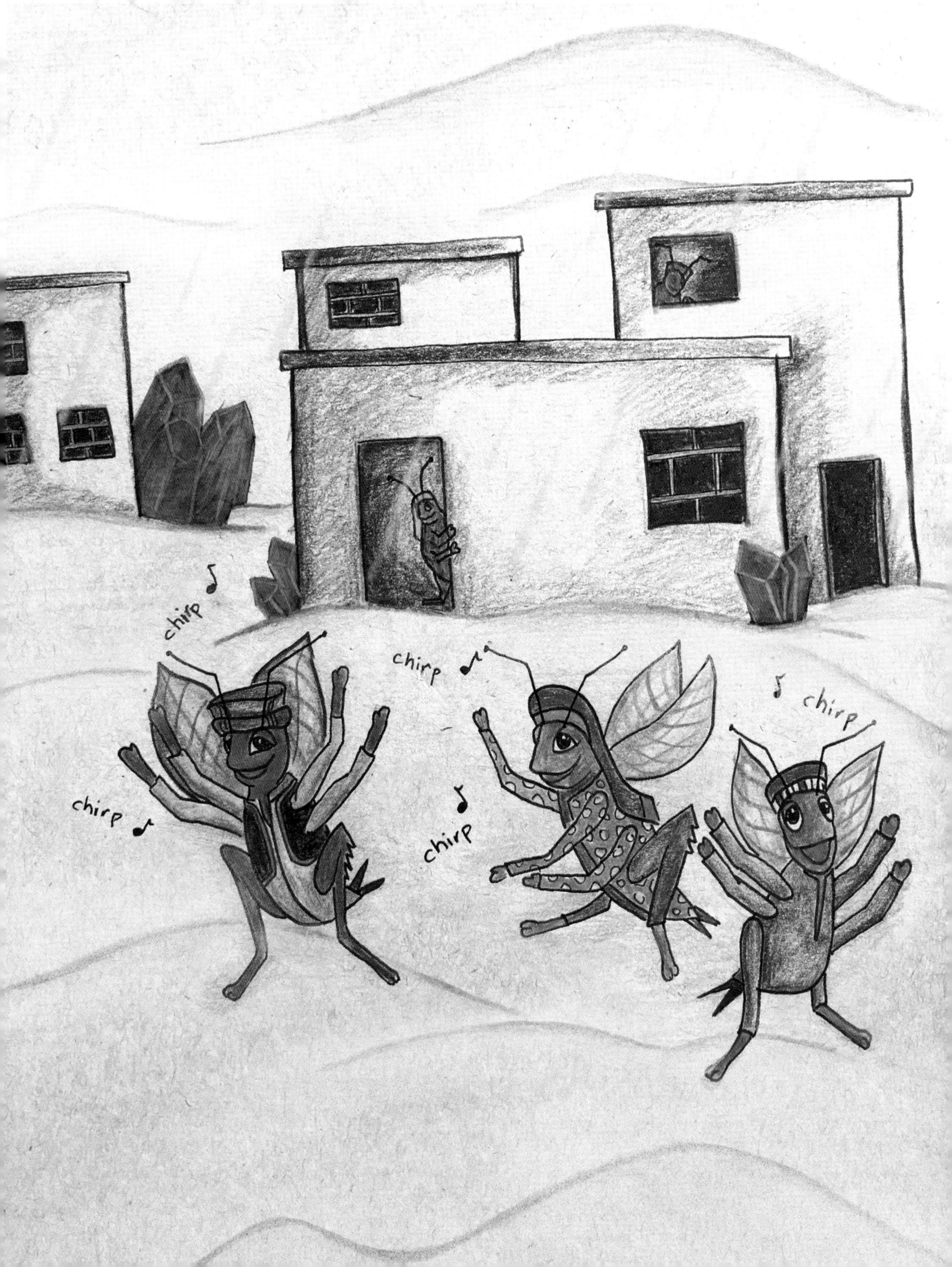
chirp
chirp
chirp
chirp
chirp

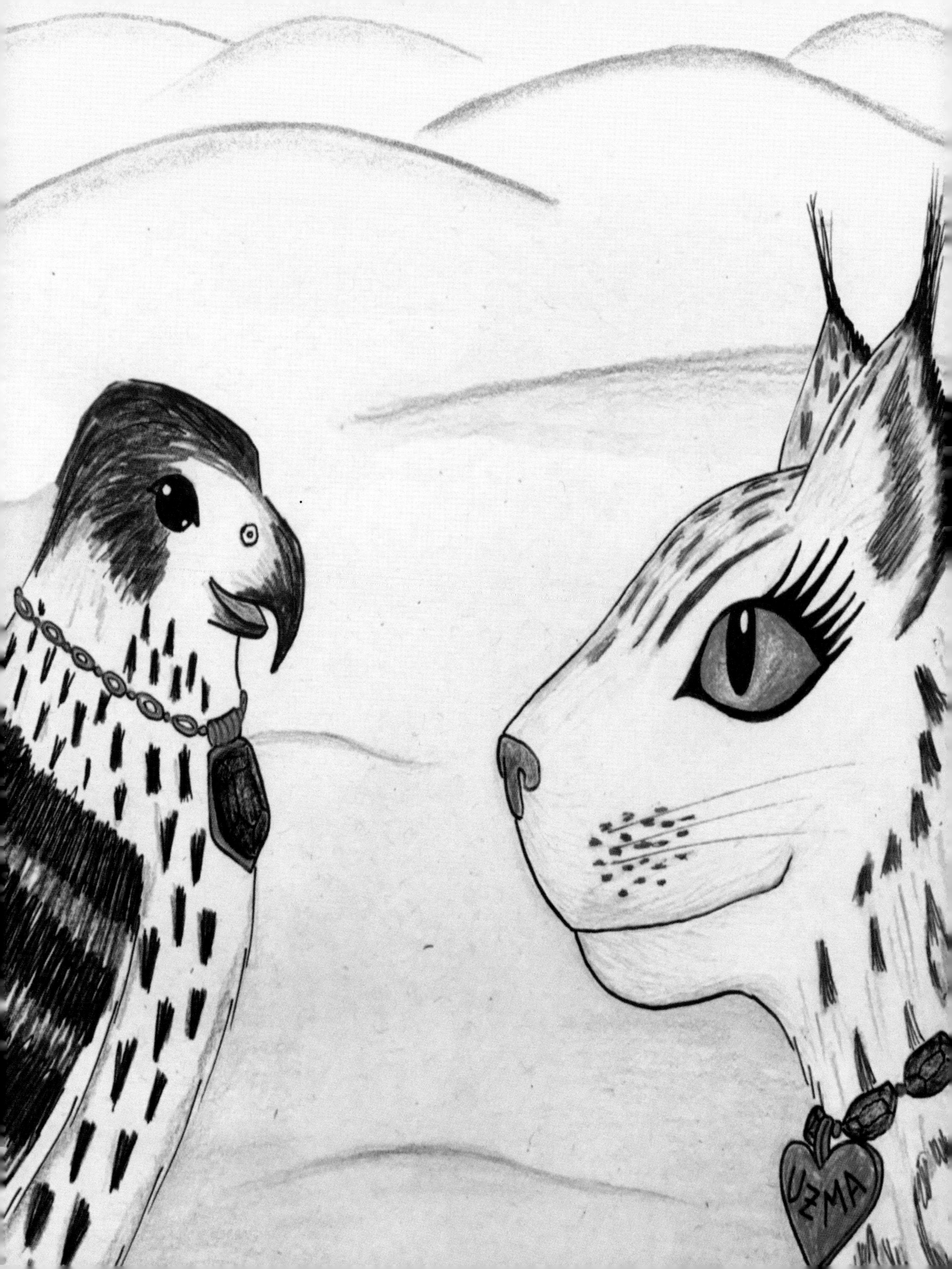
UZMA

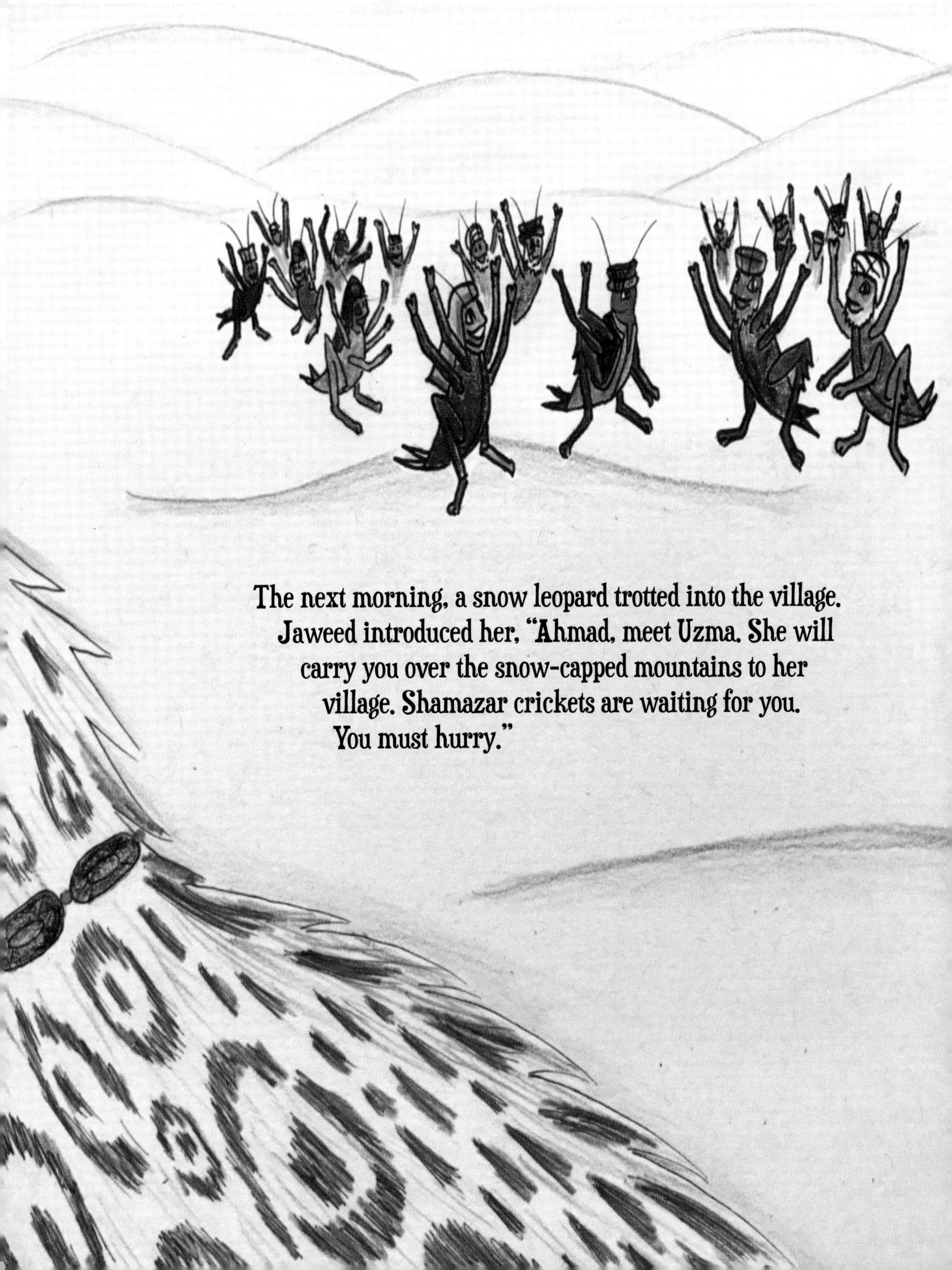

The next morning, a snow leopard trotted into the village. Jaweed introduced her, "Ahmad, meet Uzma. She will carry you over the snow-capped mountains to her village. Shamazar crickets are waiting for you. You must hurry."

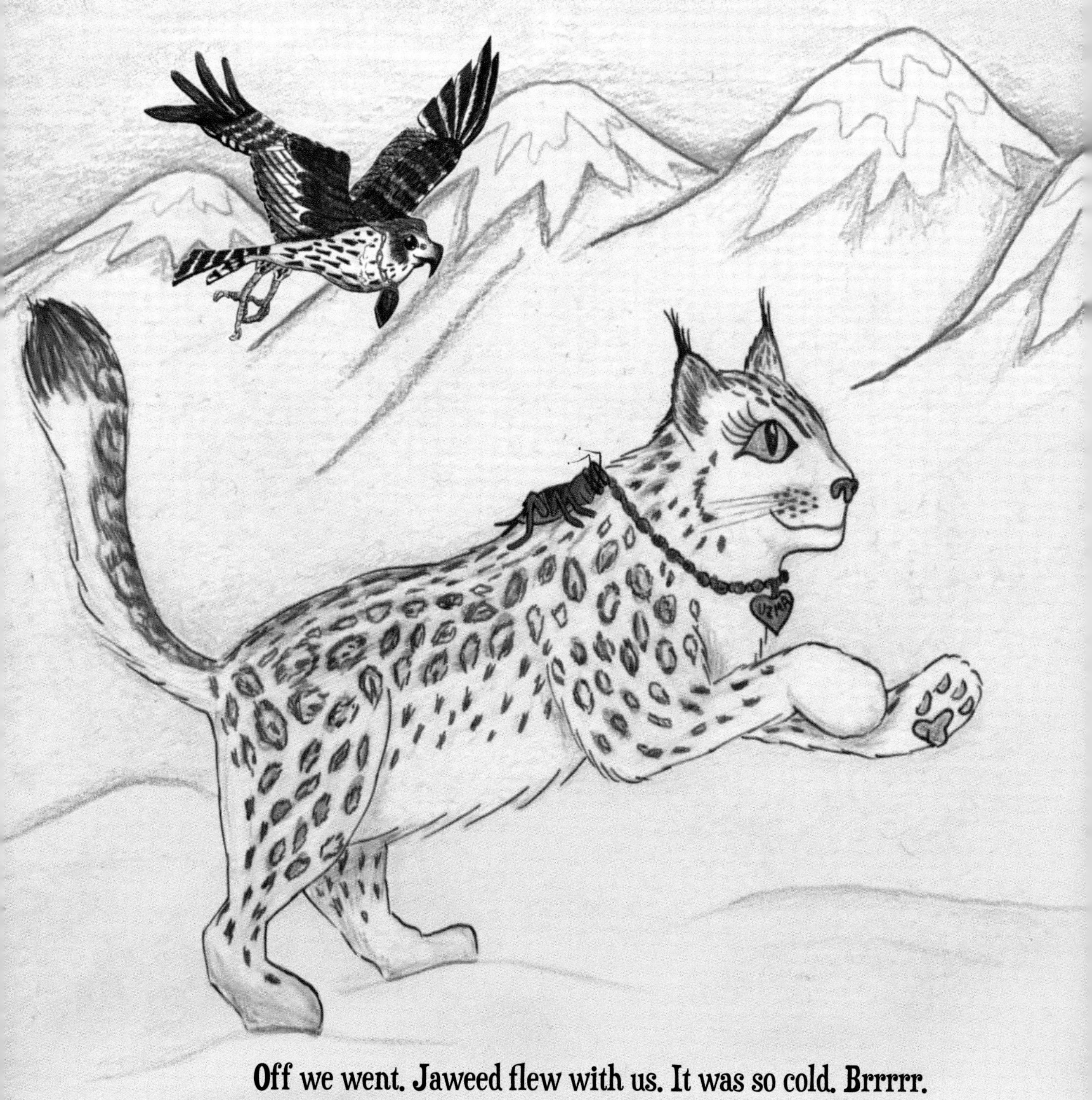
UZMA

Off we went. Jaweed flew with us. It was so cold. Brrrrr. I snuggled under Uzma's fur as she raced towards the mountains. She ran so fast that everything looked blurry. The cold made my eyes water. So, I snuggled deeper into her fur and took another nap.

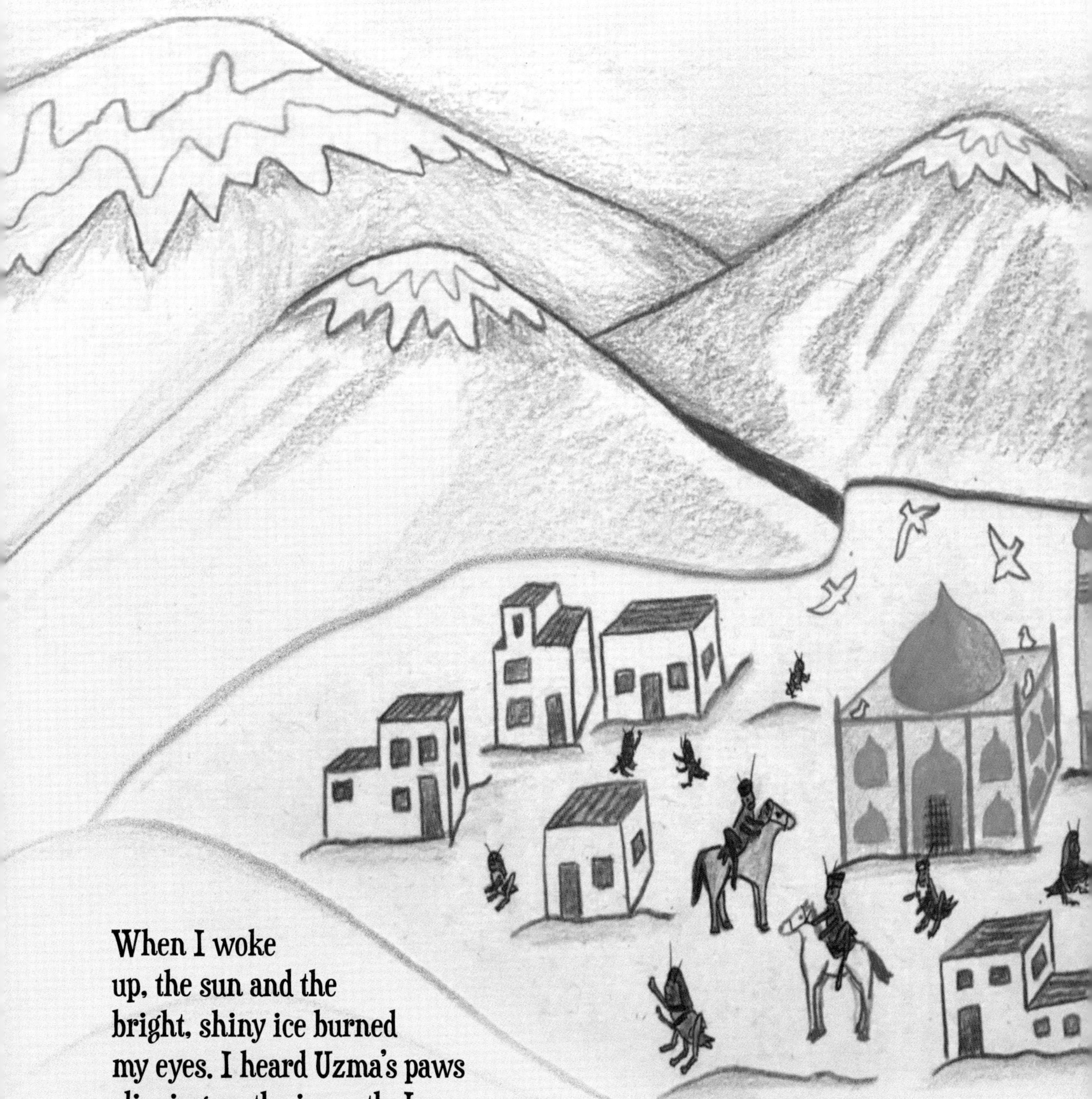

When I woke up, the sun and the bright, shiny ice burned my eyes. I heard Uzma's paws slipping on the icy path. I saw another village down the hill.

White birds—hundreds of them—flew this way and that. There were crickets on horses, too!

Soon we arrived in Shamazar. One cricket on a nice horse galloped up beside us. Uzma chuffed, alarmed at first, and then purred. I heard "ghiii-ghiii-ghiii." Looking up, I saw Jaweed soaring high above. "We've been waiting for you. We must work fast!" Mati, the village leader, said.

Mati dashed off to gather the village crickets. I taught them every cricket song in the books. Soon, every cricket in Shamazar was chirping and hopping around.

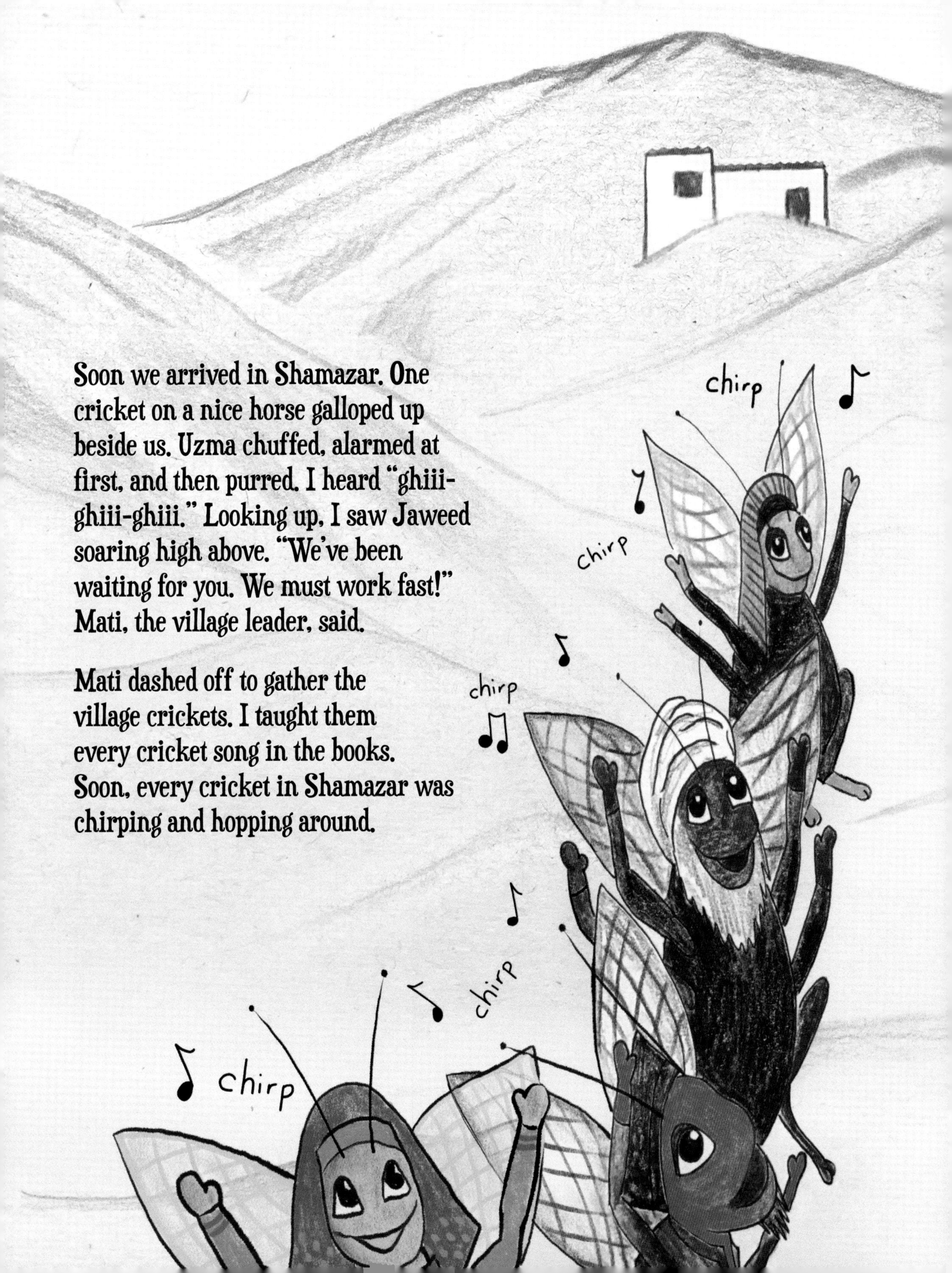
chirp
chirp
chirp
chirp
chirp

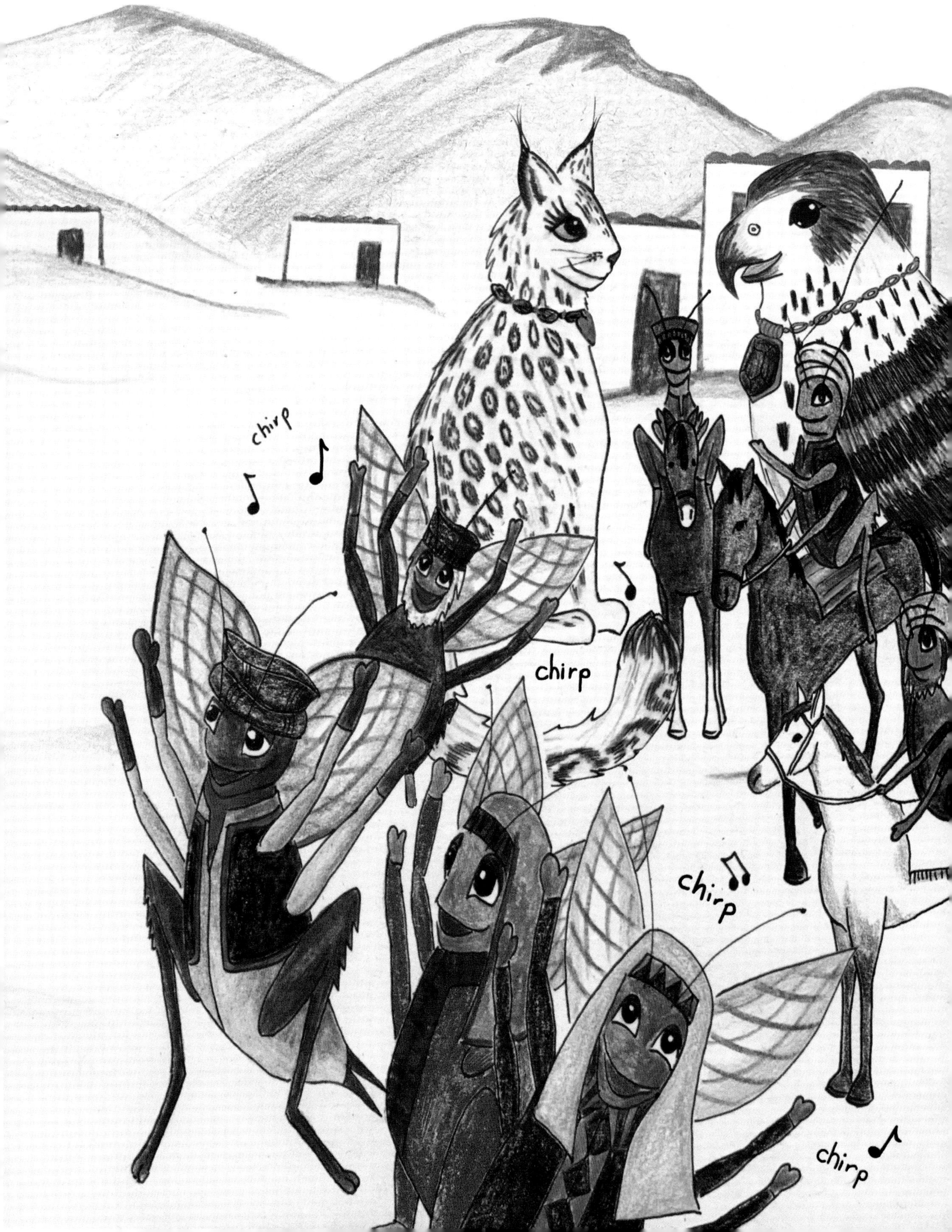
chirp
chirp
chirp
chirp

Mati jumped, "I have an idea! You go one way. We'll go another. With Jaweed's help, we'll find cricket clans. If we work together, we can teach more crickets to chirp. Every cricket chirping at the same time will make the sky happy. Clouds will breathe in the water. Rain will fall again."

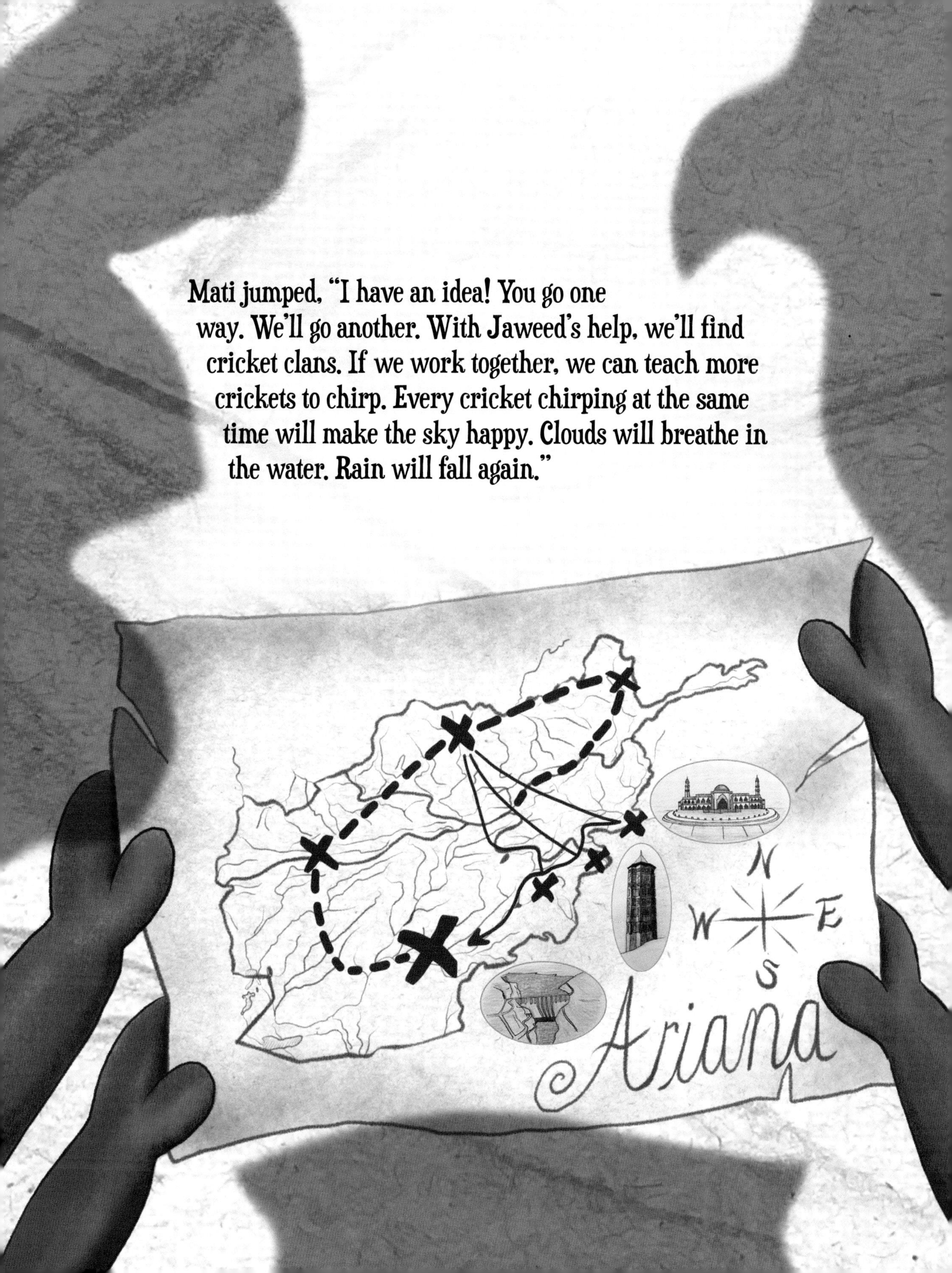
N
W
E
S
Ariana

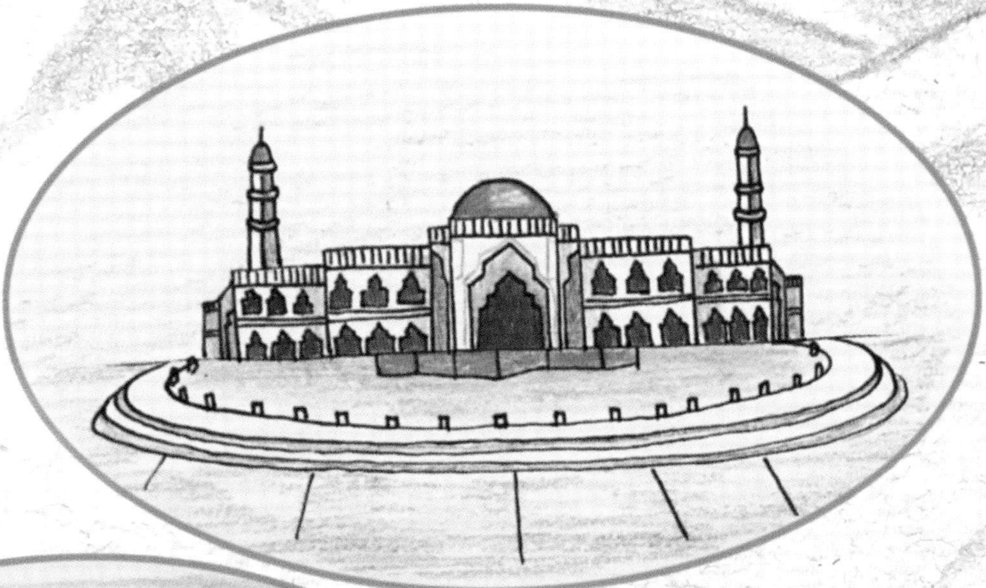

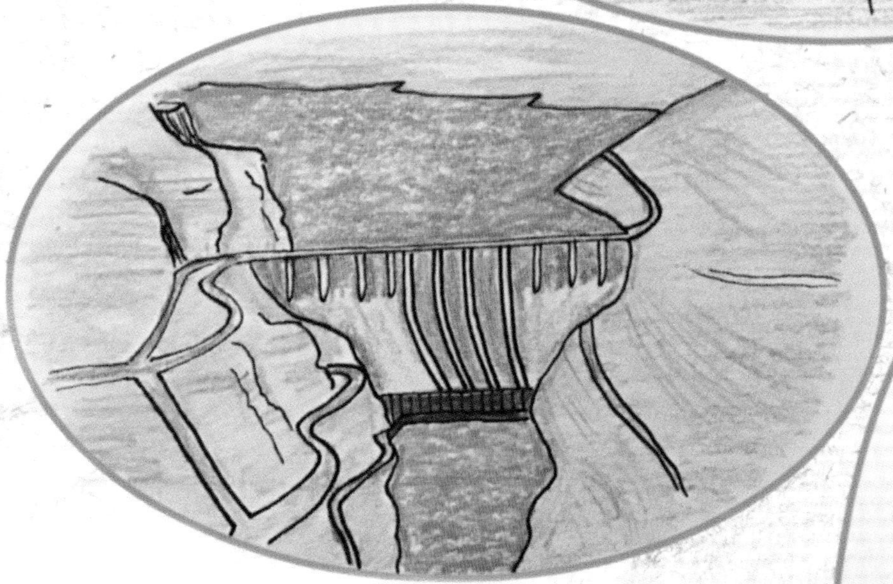

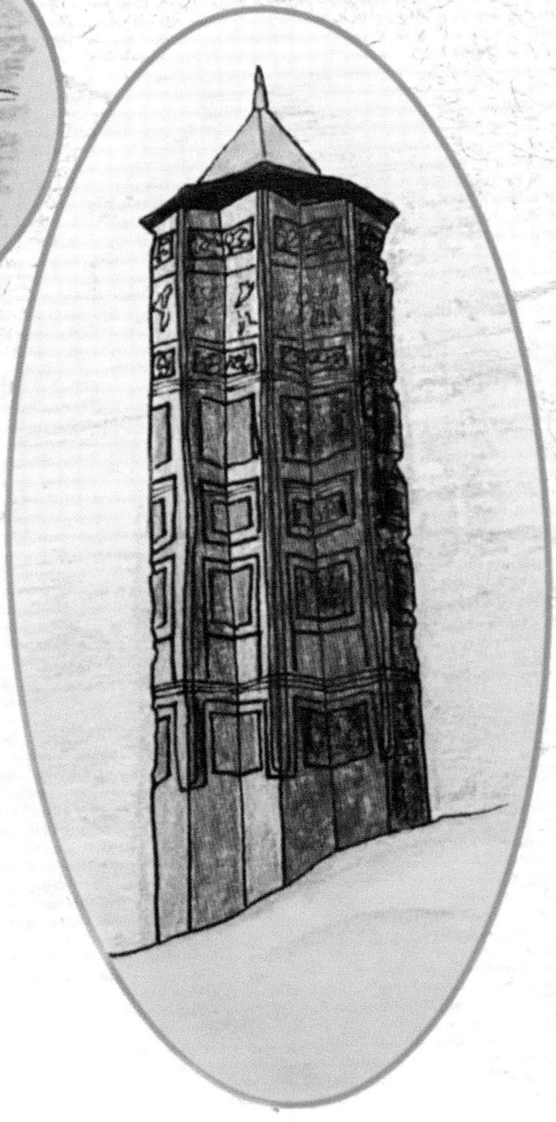

We had a plan. Mati and the others would head south, then west, and teach every cricket to chirp. Those crickets would then teach every cricket they knew to chirp. And, so on and so on and so on. My friends rode into the sunset. Jaweed flew higher until I couldn't see him anymore.

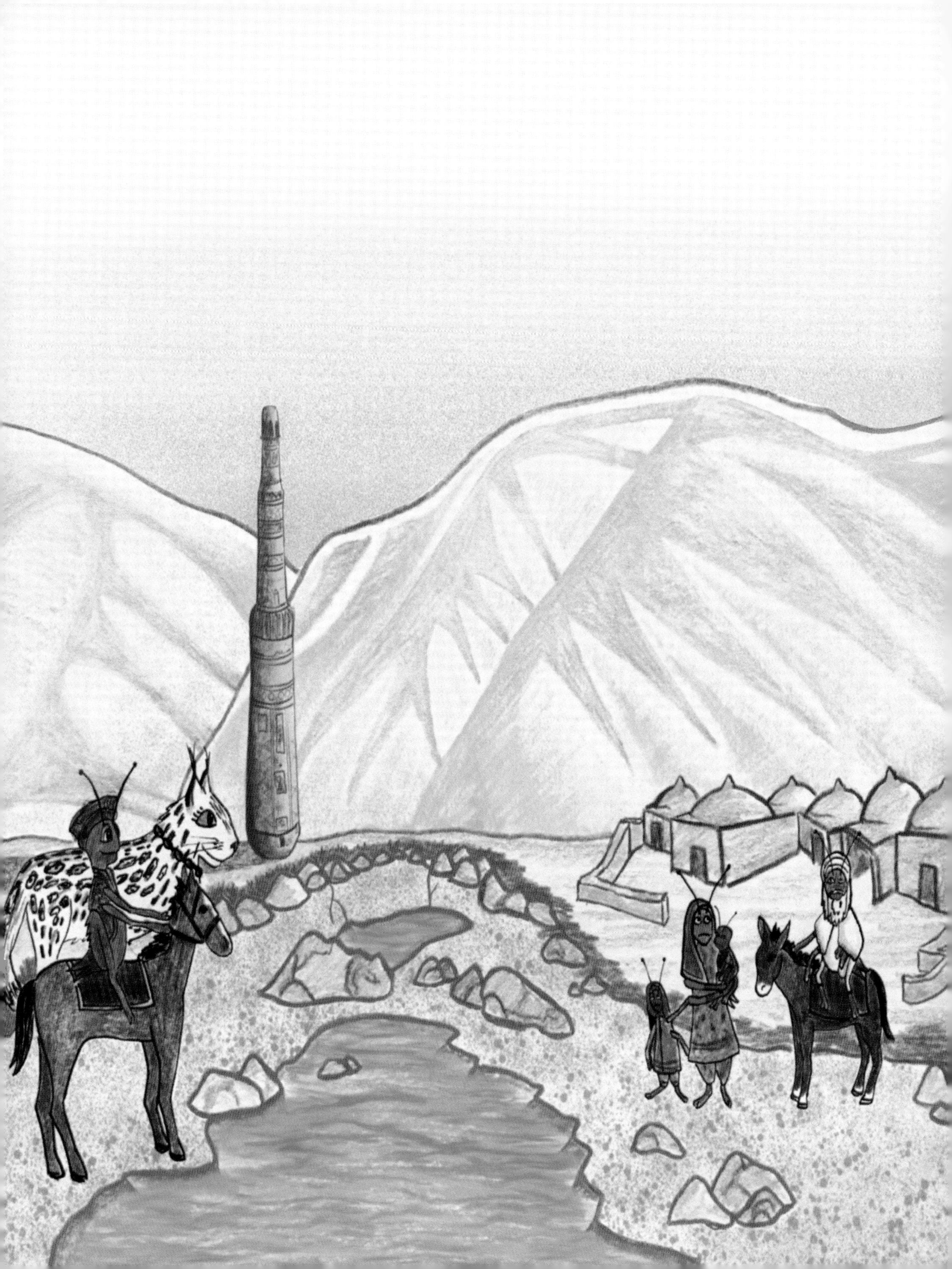

I headed west, with Uzma and Buzkh, my new horse. I felt a little lonely, leaving my friends. I was excited, too. We planned to meet again in Arachosia, the very best place to watch the day turn to night in the middle of the day, causing crickets to chirp. I was on my way to find a place where two rivers met at a lake. Crickets gathered there for the water.

We saw a village with round rooftops and a tall tower. We found the lake. A family was there to have a picnic. They were sad because the water was low. "I remember when it was overflowing with beautiful blue water," the nice cricket mother cried. "We need rain."

I said, "I know how to make it rain! Calling all crickets, young and old! I'll teach you to chirp again. Once you start chirping, clouds will fill up and rain will fall down. Lakes will rise. Rivers will flow. Mountains will be covered with snow. Waterfalls will freeze in place and wait for spring to show. Gather your families here. Together, we will chirp again!"

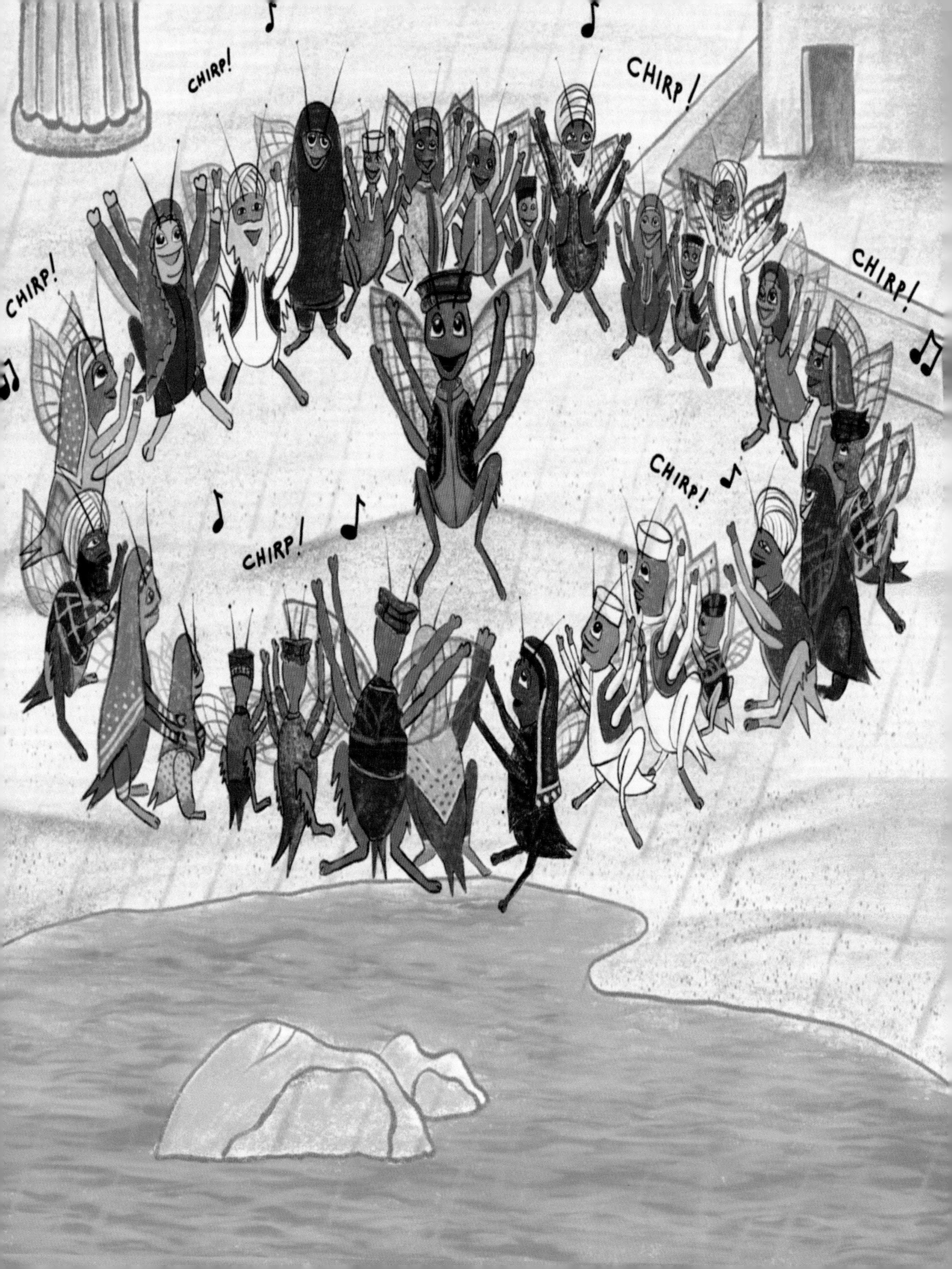
CHIRP!
CHIRP!
CHIRP!
CHIRP!
CHIRP!
CHIRP!

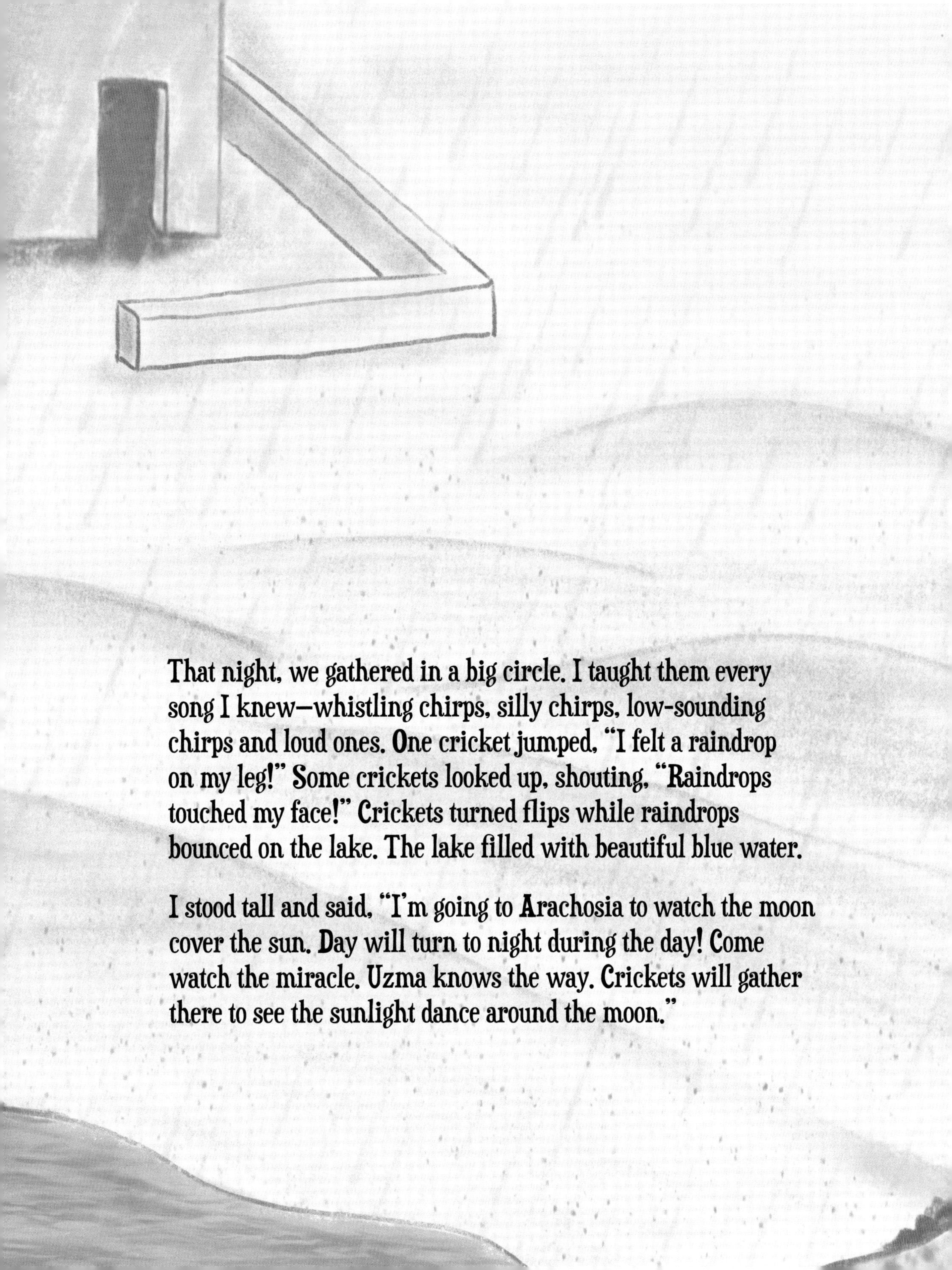

That night, we gathered in a big circle. I taught them every song I knew—whistling chirps, silly chirps, low-sounding chirps and loud ones. One cricket jumped, "I felt a raindrop on my leg!" Some crickets looked up, shouting, "Raindrops touched my face!" Crickets turned flips while raindrops bounced on the lake. The lake filled with beautiful blue water.

I stood tall and said, "I'm going to Arachosia to watch the moon cover the sun. Day will turn to night during the day! Come watch the miracle. Uzma knows the way. Crickets will gather there to see the sunlight dance around the moon."

Meanwhile, Mati, Jaweed, and the others saw many curious places. A giant statue carved in the side of a mountain. A river, high on one side and low on the other. In one place, a tall, perfectly round tower that rose up to the sky. They taught crickets they met along the way to chirp. Many crickets followed them, too.

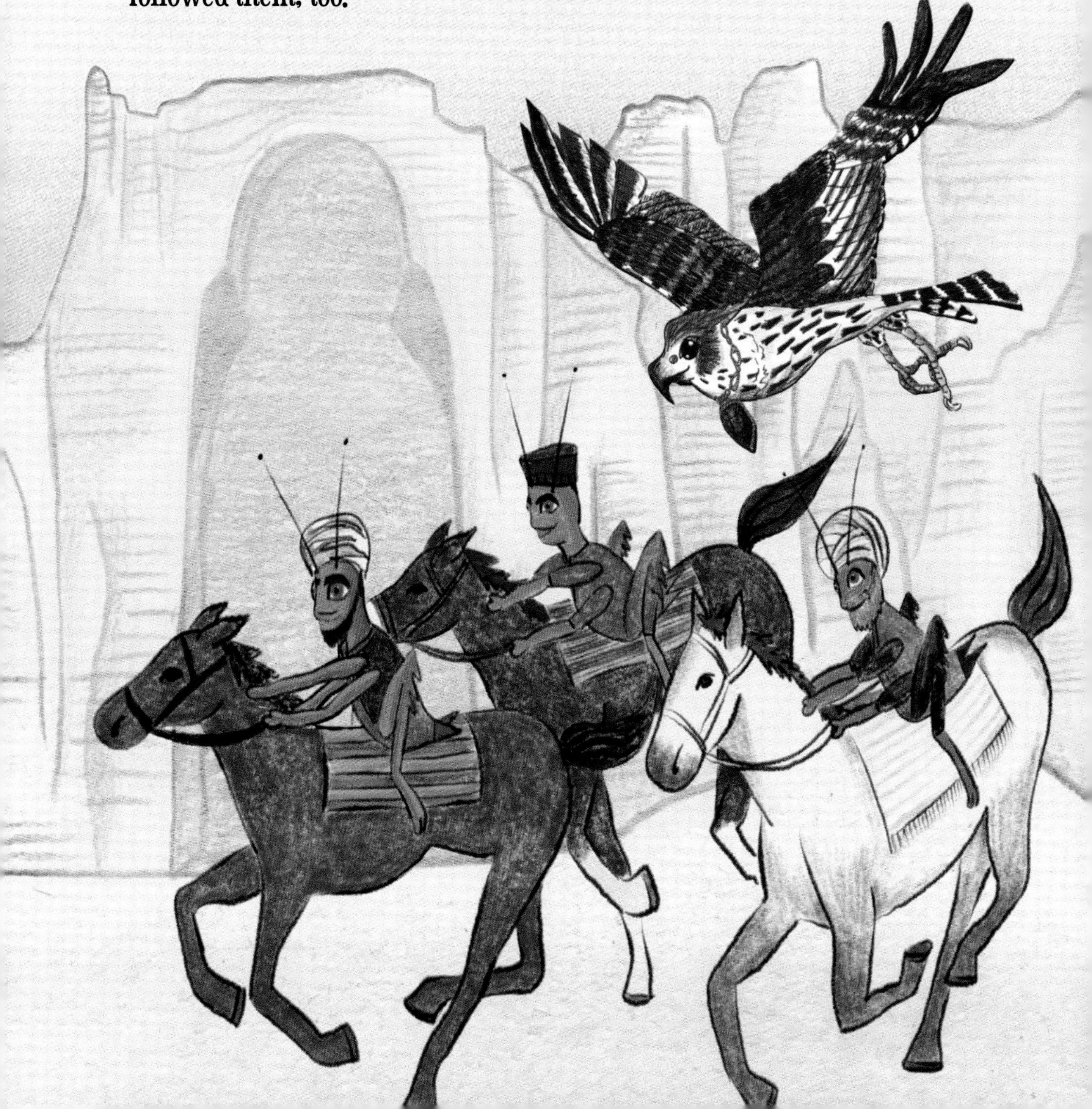

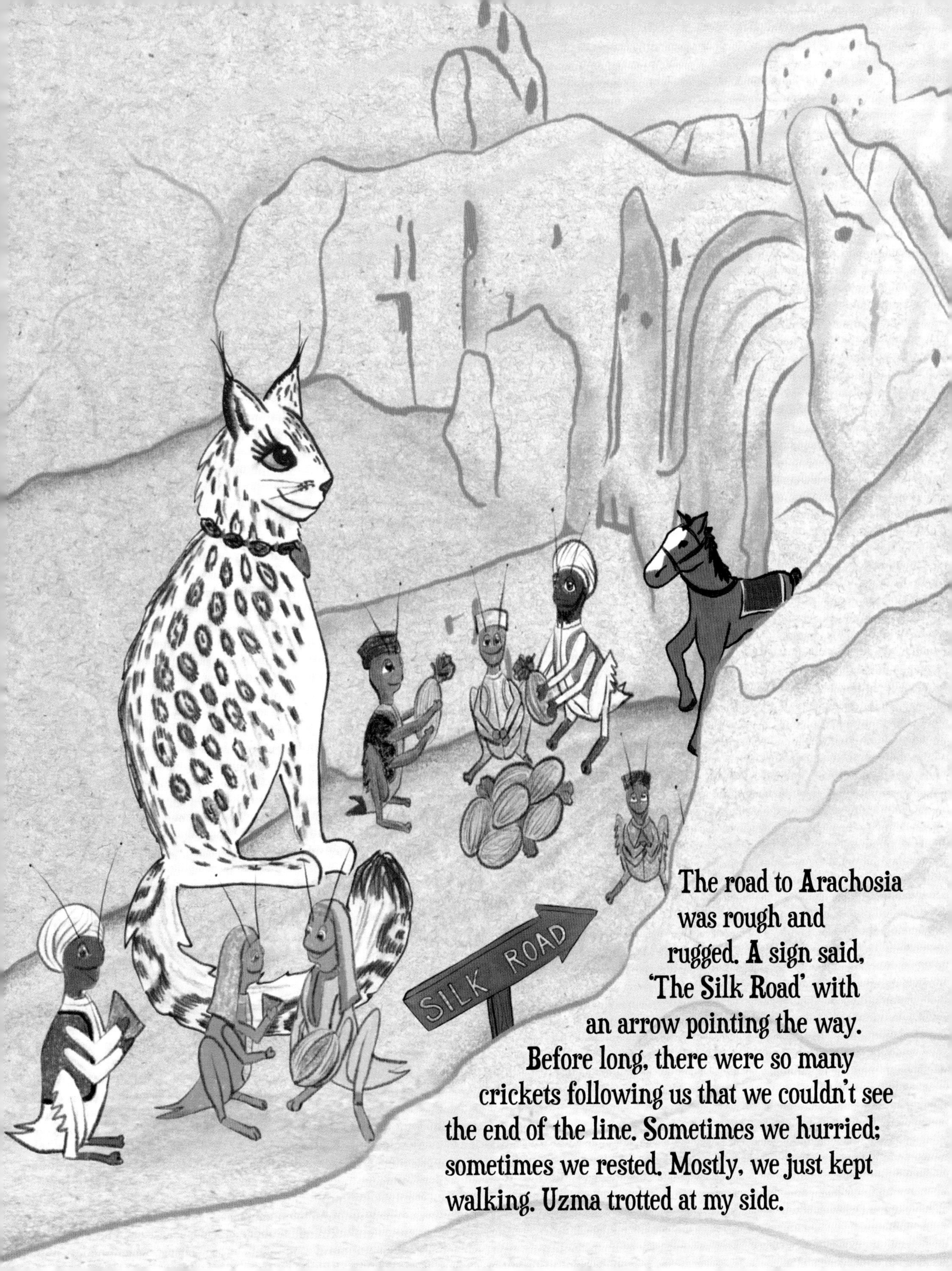
SILK ROAD

The road to Arachosia was rough and rugged. A sign said, 'The Silk Road' with an arrow pointing the way. Before long, there were so many crickets following us that we couldn't see the end of the line. Sometimes we hurried; sometimes we rested. Mostly, we just kept walking. Uzma trotted at my side.

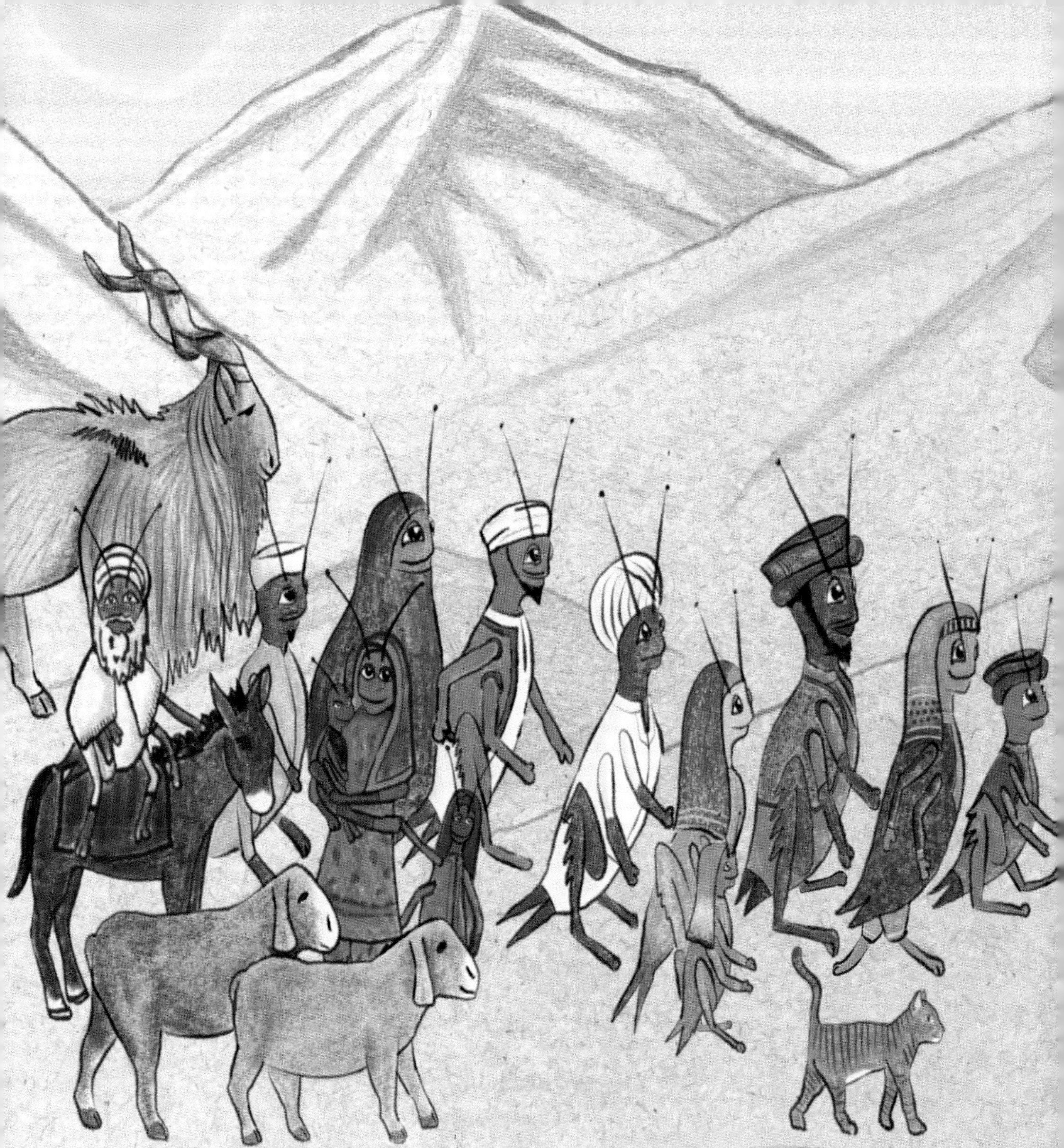

We passed a building where crickets were outside playing a game. They wore blue uniforms and waved white paddles in the air. As we watched, a swarm of crickets ran towards us. Some of the crickets with me were scared and hid in the dirt.

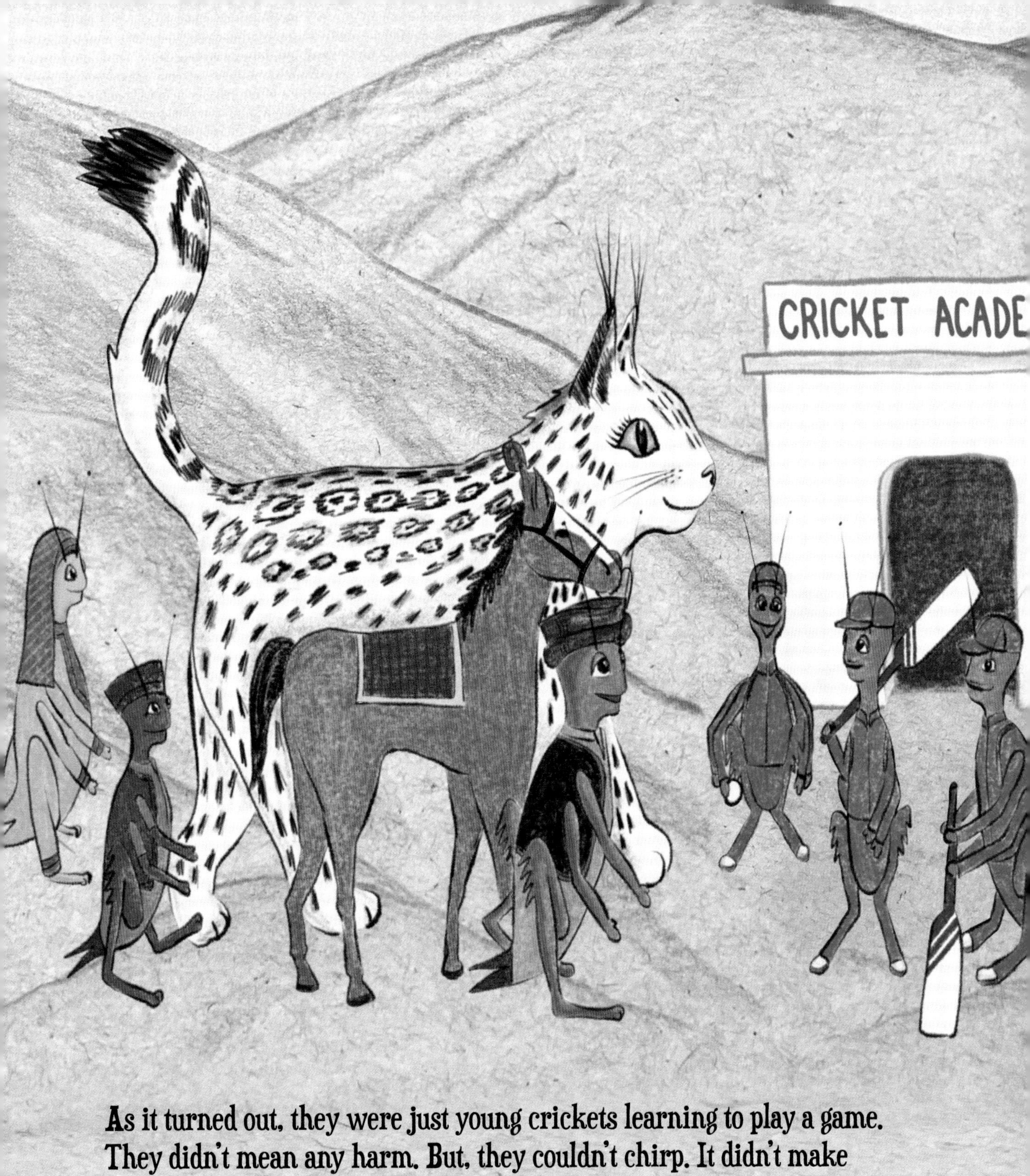
CRICKET ACADE

As it turned out, they were just young crickets learning to play a game. They didn't mean any harm. But, they couldn't chirp. It didn't make sense to me. "Cricket Academy crickets couldn't chirp?" I wondered about that. I told them about the big event and taught them how to chirp, too. They came with us. We marched on.

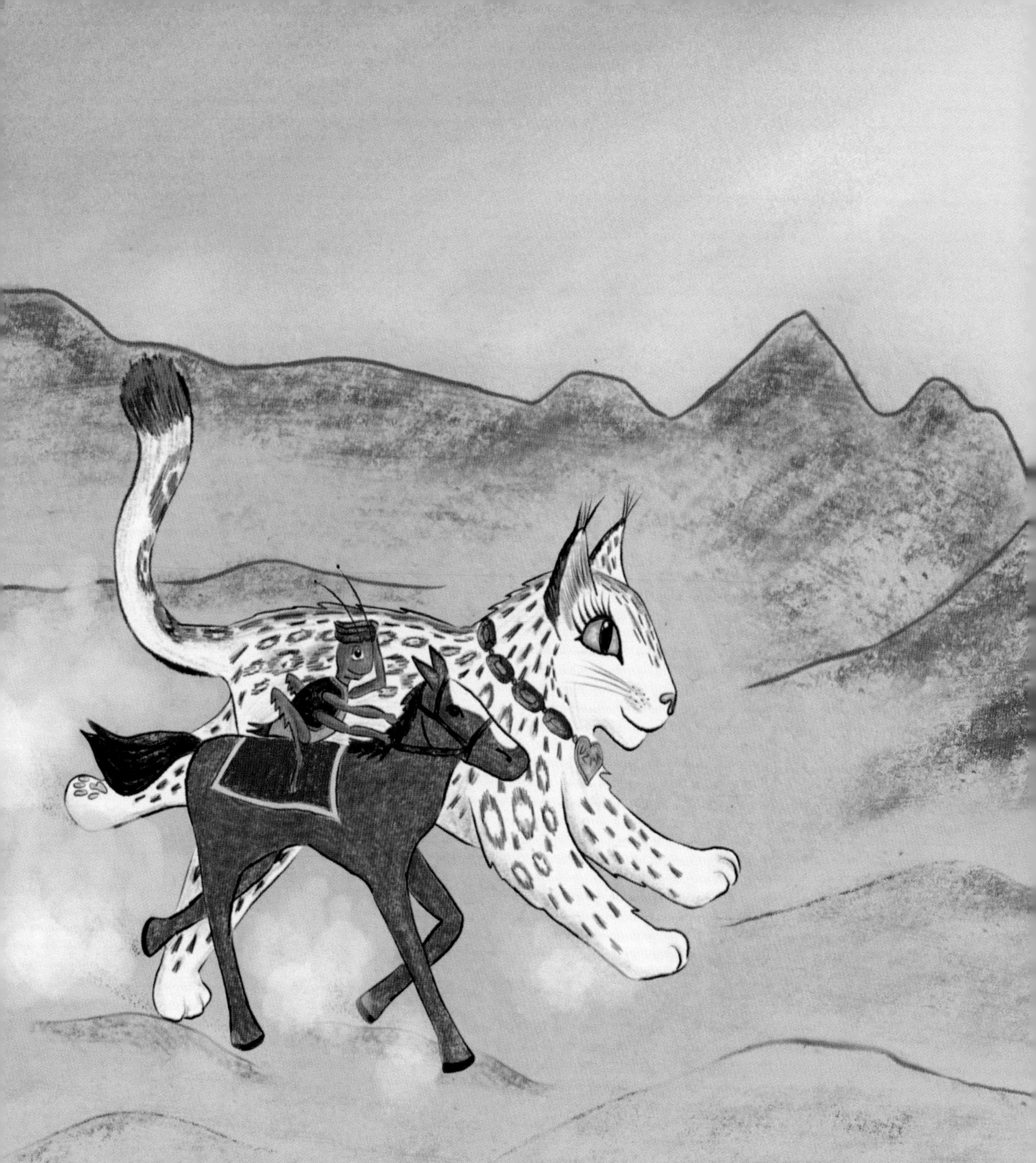

The next morning, the day of the miracle, Arachosia sparkled bright in the distance. Cricket clans marched together towards the beautiful city.

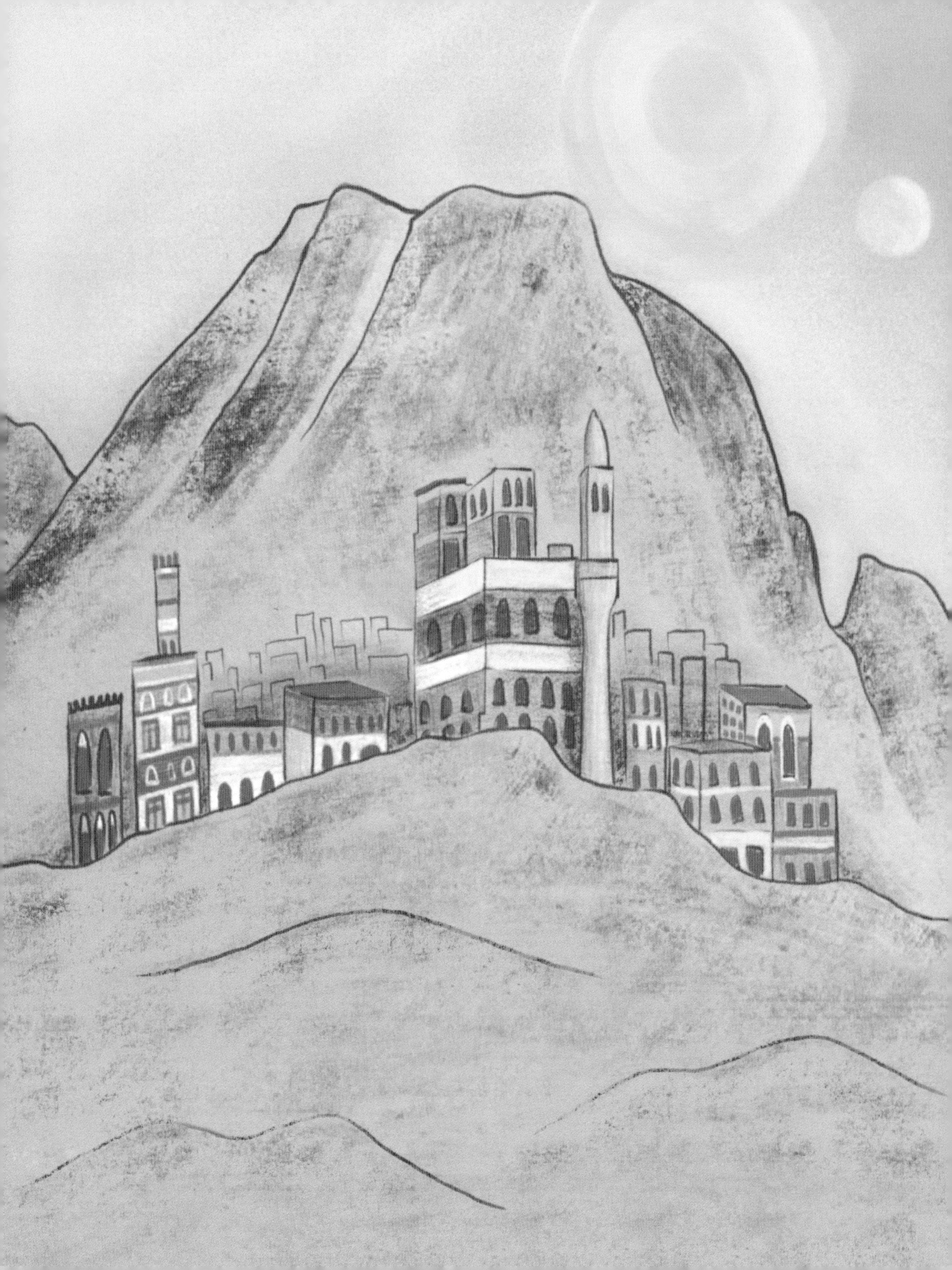

We gathered in the town square.
I saw a bright red, round fruit in one store window. A pomegranate!

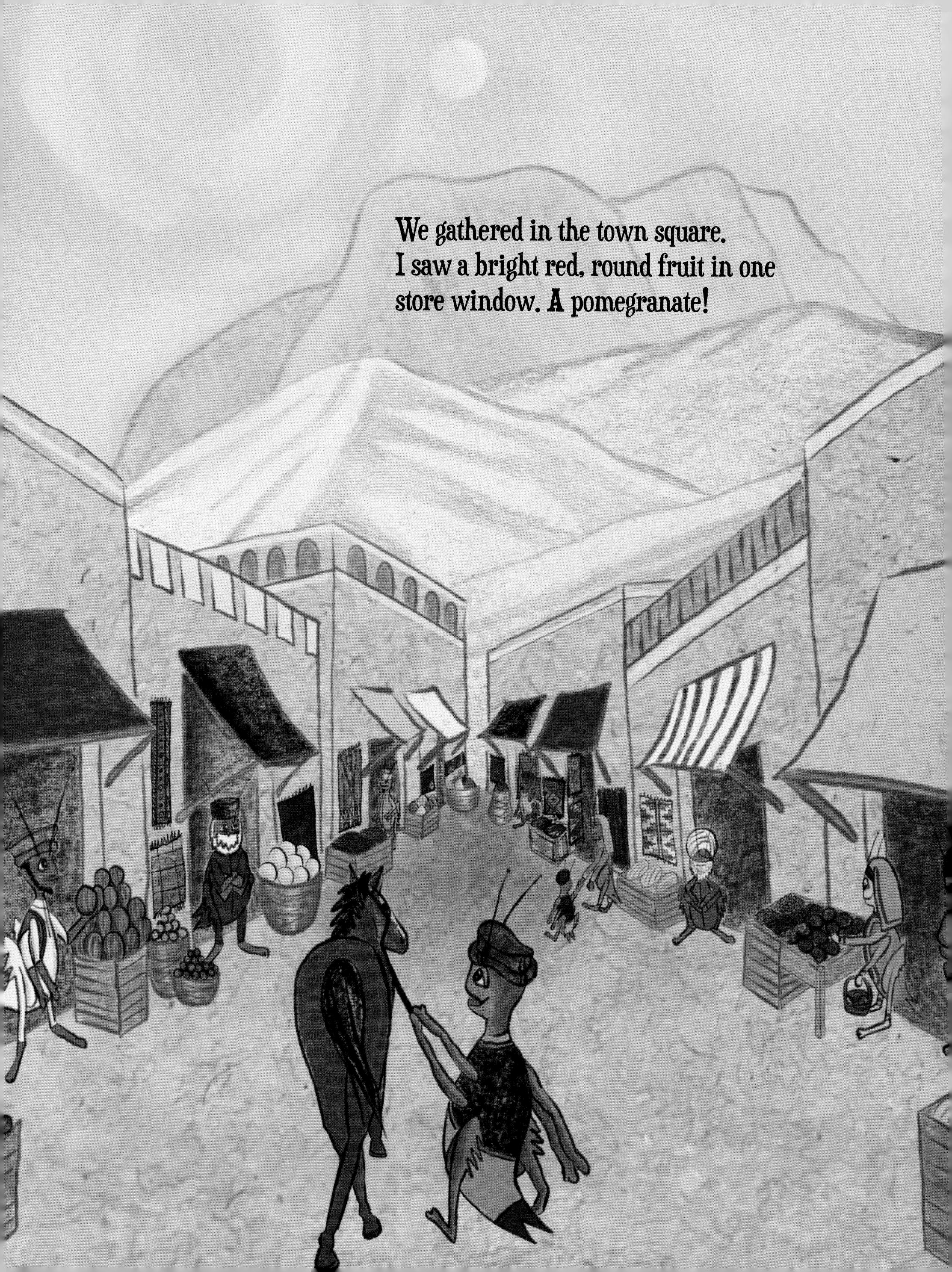

Reaching for the fruit, I heard a sweet voice say, "My father grew that pomegranate." I blinked, gulped, and opened my eyes. She was the loveliest cricket I ever saw. She said, "I'm Zuhra. And, you're the one who will save our land."

We walked around together. I told her where I'd been, the things I'd seen, and the crickets I'd met. See children, that cricket Zuhra? She's your Grandmother. We've been together since that day. Back to the story though. . ...

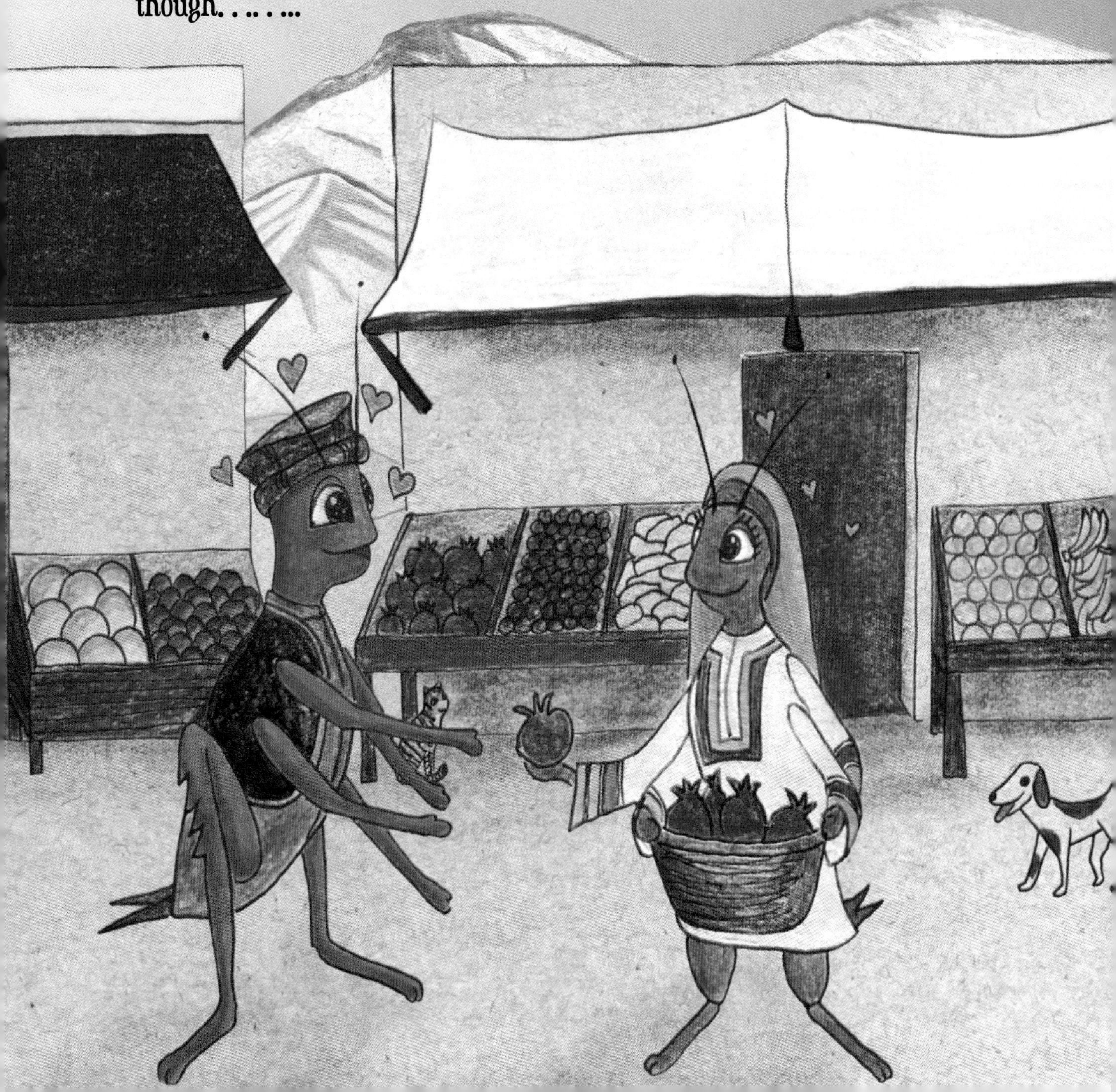

Later that day, the town square filled with crickets. So many crickets were jumping around. Some who had already learned how were chirping at the top of their cricket lungs. I shouted, "Calling all crickets. Gather around to learn to chirp. There's no time to waste."

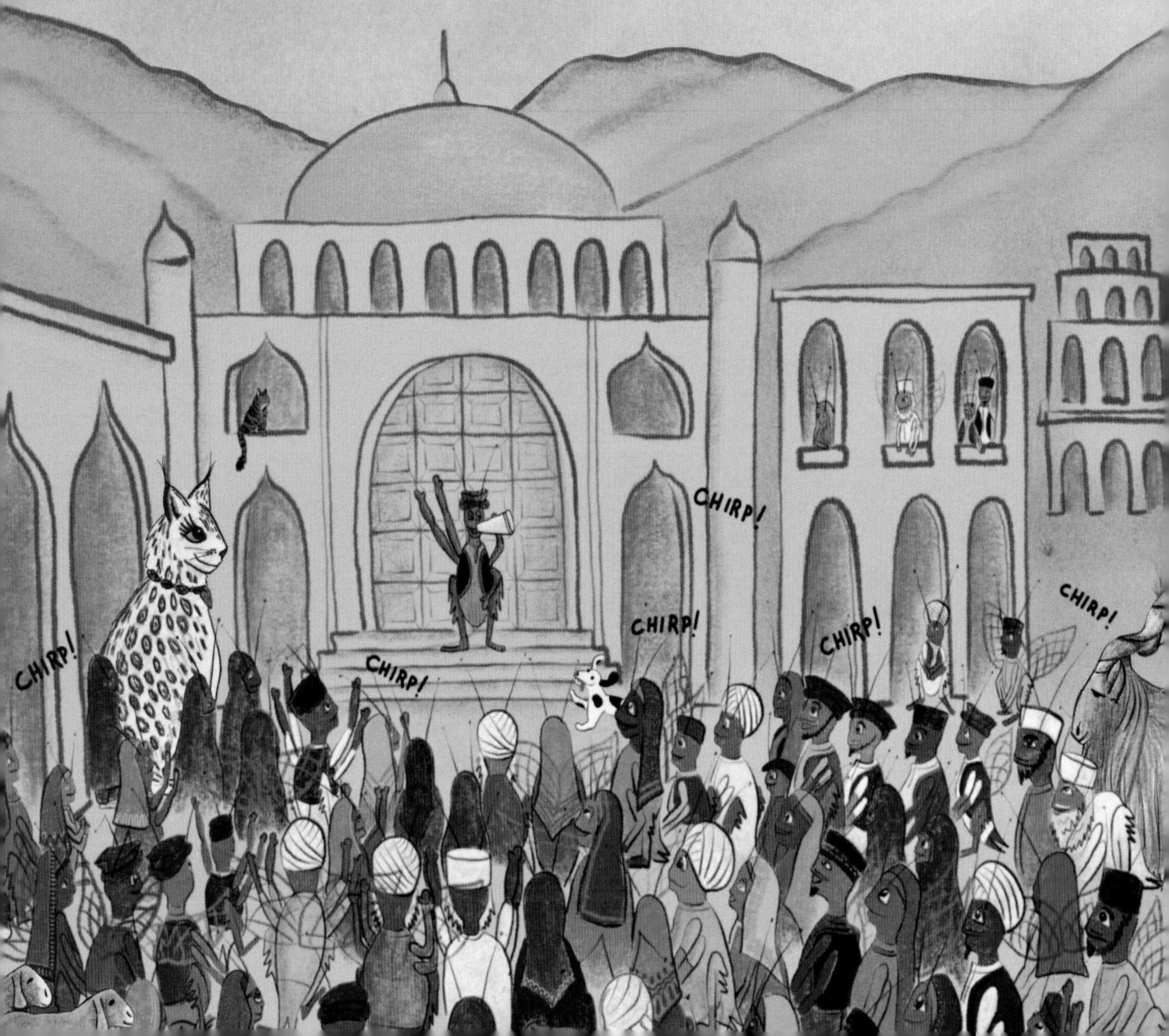
CHIRP!
CHIRP!
CHIRP!
CHIRP!
CHIRP!
CHIRP!

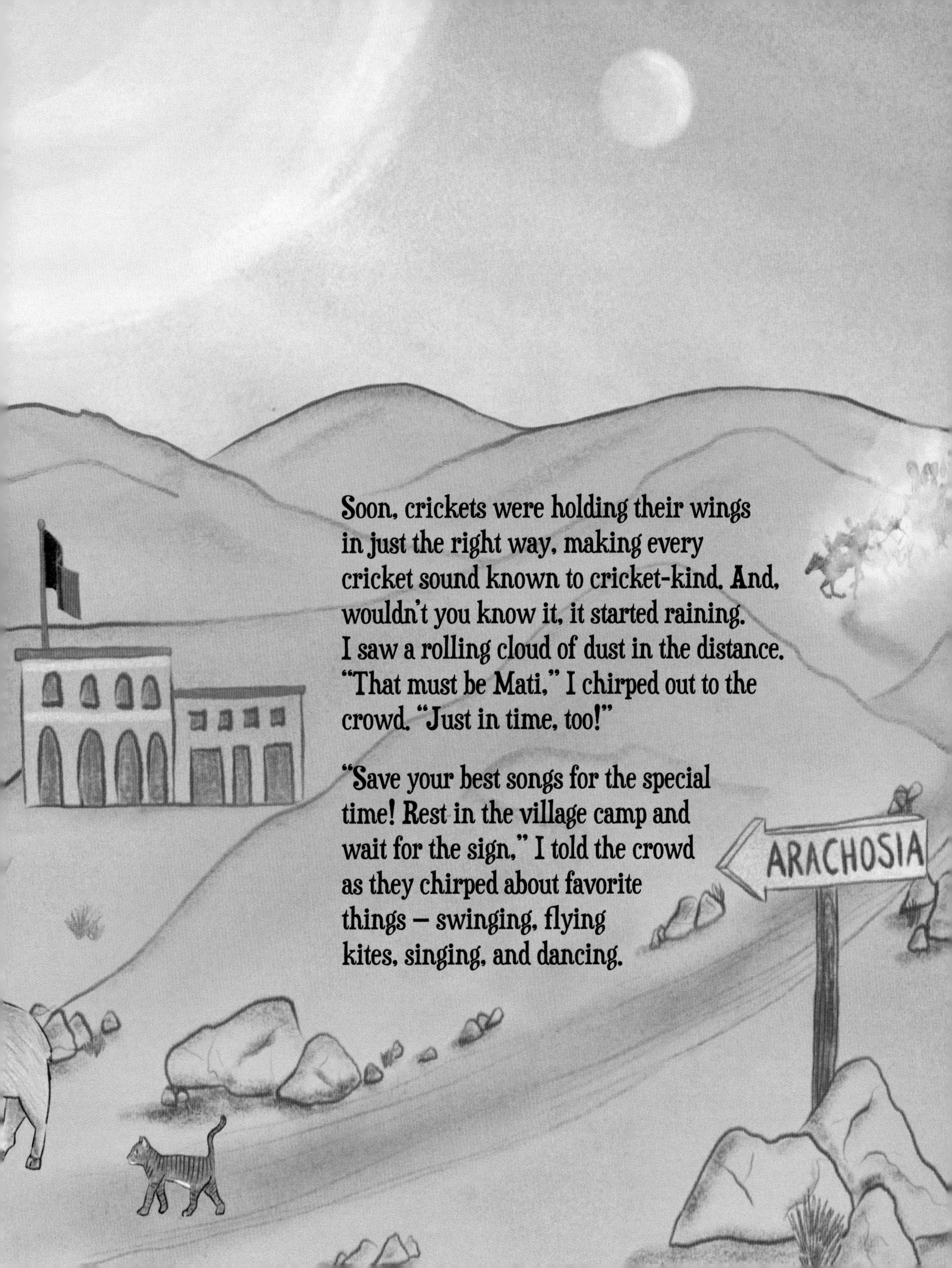
ARACHOSIA

Soon, crickets were holding their wings in just the right way, making every cricket sound known to cricket-kind. And, wouldn't you know it, it started raining. I saw a rolling cloud of dust in the distance. "That must be Mati," I chirped out to the crowd. "Just in time, too!"

"Save your best songs for the special time! Rest in the village camp and wait for the sign," I told the crowd as they chirped about favorite things – swinging, flying kites, singing, and dancing.

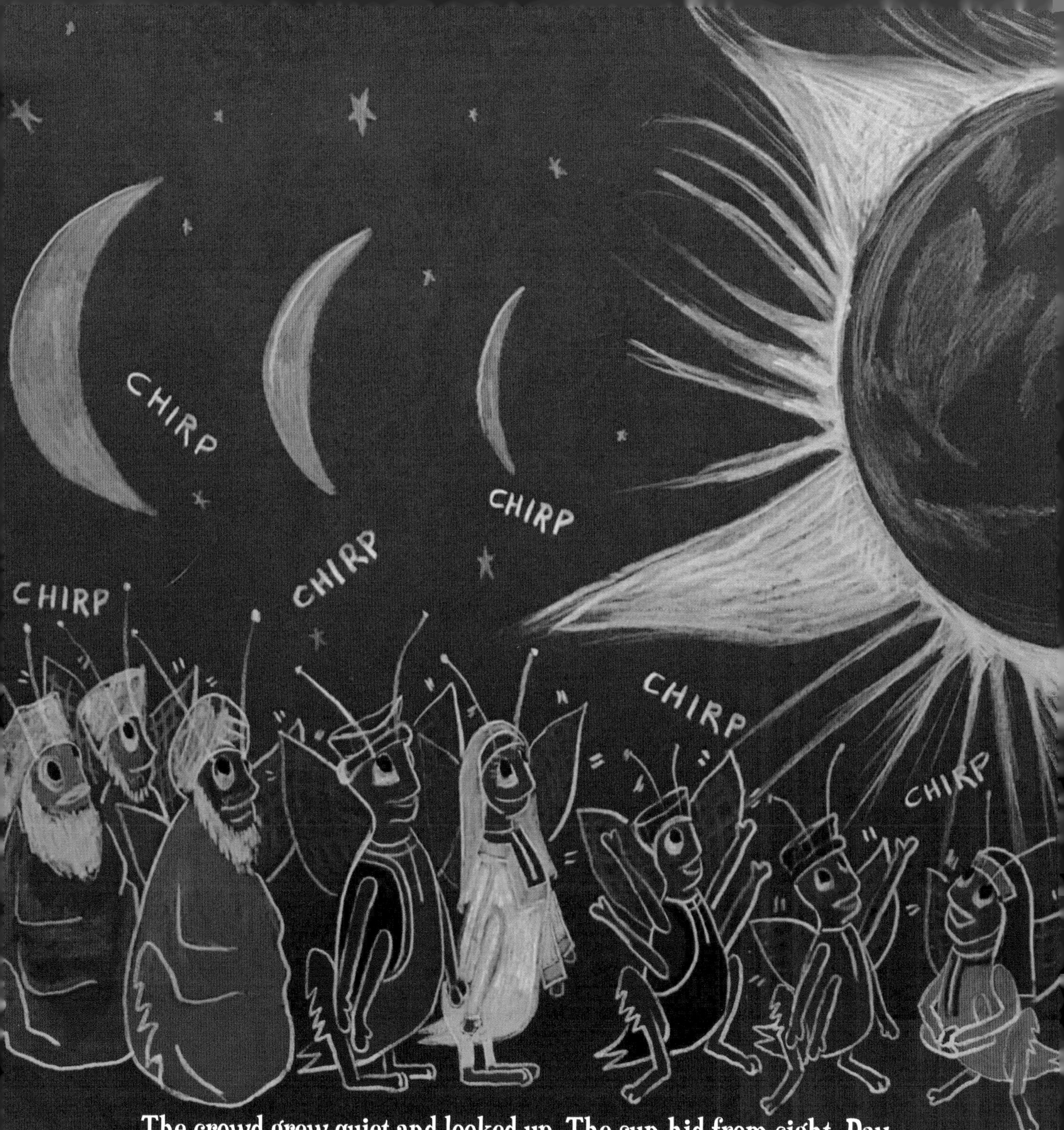
CHIRP
CHIRP
CHIRP
CHIRP
CHIRP
CHIRP

The crowd grew quiet and looked up. The sun hid from sight. Day turned to night. Birds took flight. Then, one by one, crickets started chirping. At first, only soft chirps and short chirps. One cricket belted out a loud, fancy chirp. Crickets started jumping and chirping. "Look at that. Magnificent. Amazing. Beautiful. A miracle!" The chirping crowd grew louder and louder still. Every cricket song ever heard echoed across the land. Raindrops fell from the sky.

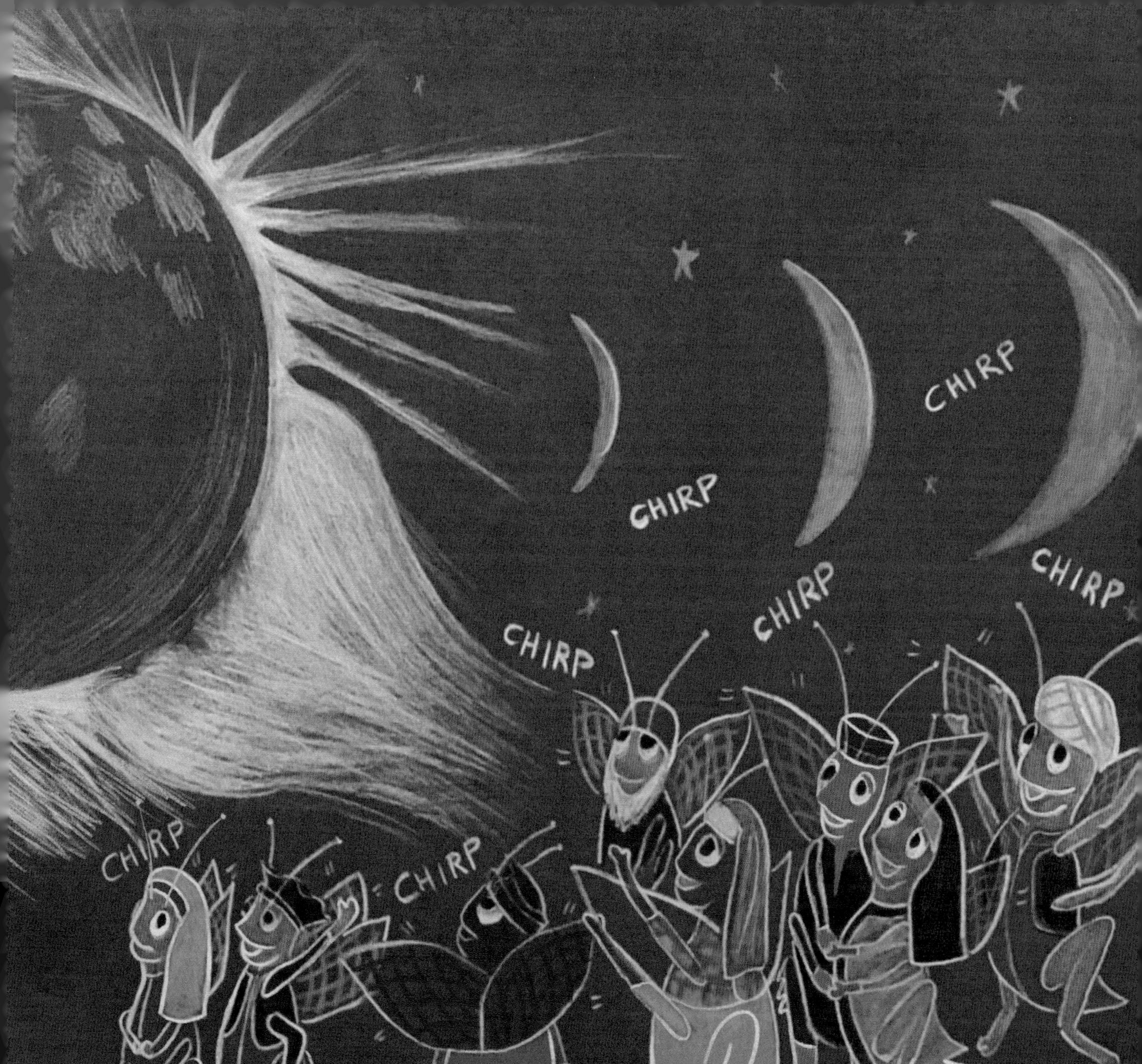
CHIRP
CHIRP
CHIRP
CHIRP
CHIRP
CHIRP
CHIRP

Without any warning at all, the sun peeked out from the other side of the moon! "Ooohs" and "Ahhhs" were heard between the chirps and trills. "The diamond ring!" they shouted with joy! It happened so fast! Once the sun tiptoed out, the night turned back into day. Strange shadows danced on the ground. And, to this day, there's never been such an ear-splitting gathering of chirping crickets.

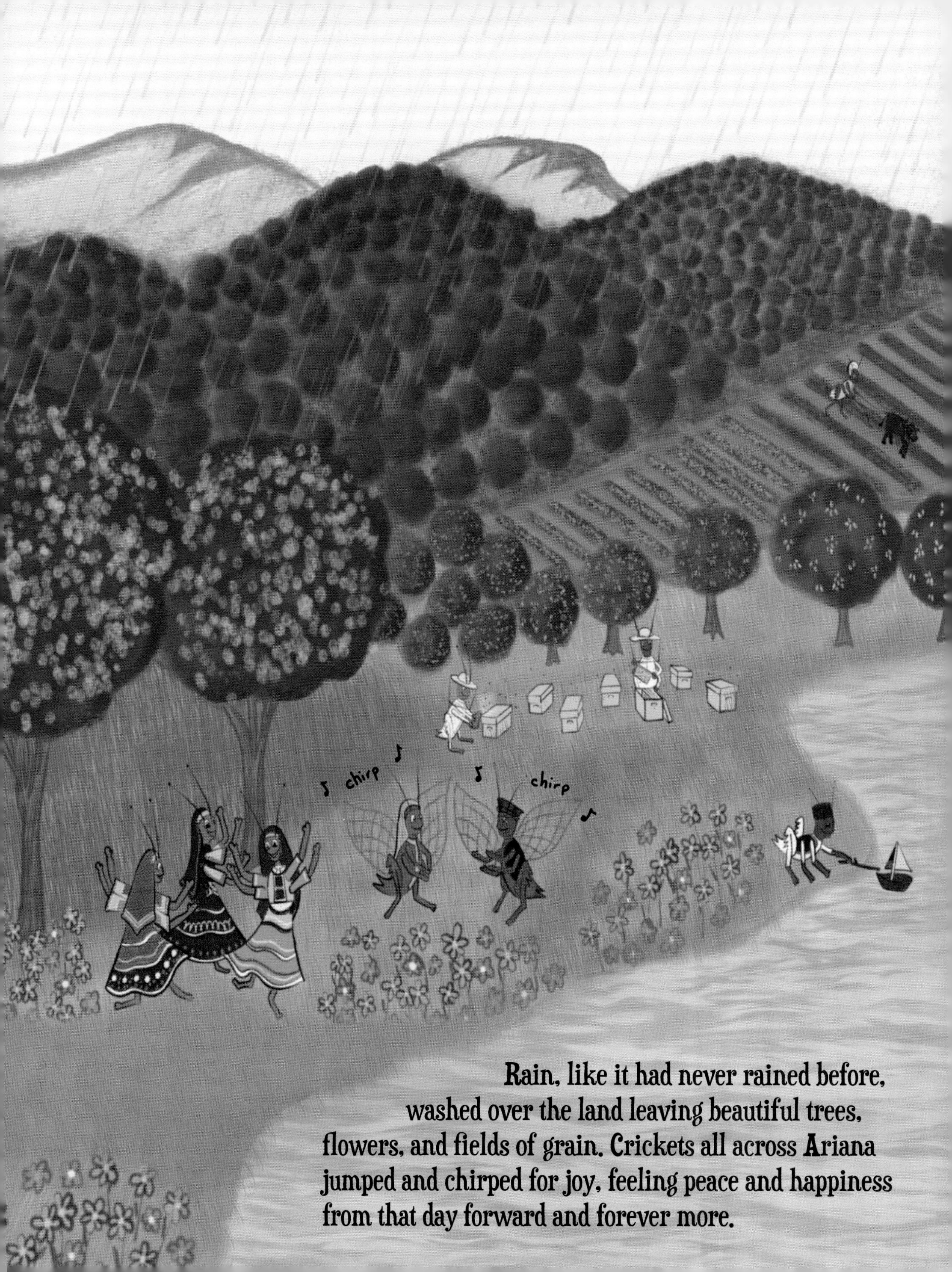
chirp
chirp

Rain, like it had never rained before, washed over the land leaving beautiful trees, flowers, and fields of grain. Crickets all across Ariana jumped and chirped for joy, feeling peace and happiness from that day forward and forever more.

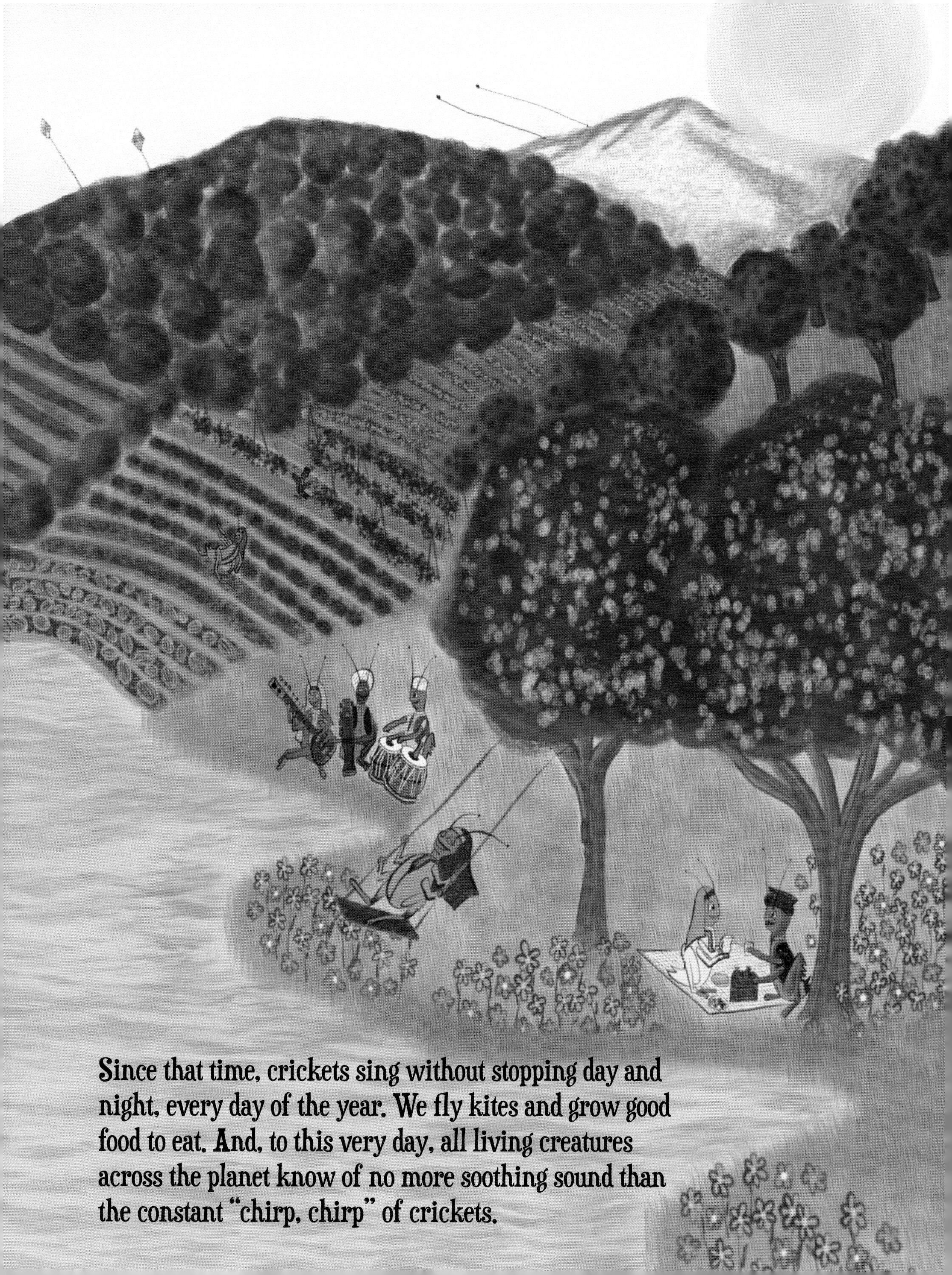

Since that time, crickets sing without stopping day and night, every day of the year. We fly kites and grow good food to eat. And, to this very day, all living creatures across the planet know of no more soothing sound than the constant "chirp, chirp" of crickets.

The most recent total solar eclipse visible across Afghanistan was on October 24, 1995; the totality would have been ideally visible over Kandahar. The next full solar eclipse to cross Afghanistan will be on March 20, 2034, with totality just north of Kandahar. I had no idea of these facts when deciding to have the story's climactic event be a full solar eclipse visible from Kandahar. An eclipse, solar or lunar, in all of its majesty, serves to elevate us, if only momentarily, above our troubles. Sharing the experience knows no religion, race, creed, political leaning or status in life. An eclipse is a gift to a riven nation. It ignites an awakening in the soul and can return the heart back to the right path.

MOONS ORBIT
MOON
SUN
EARTH

Never look at a solar eclipse without proper eye protection. The only safe way to view a Sun's eclipse is through special-purpose solar filters, such as ISO 12312-2 international safety eclipse glasses or handheld solar viewers. An alternative method is indirect via pinhole projection.

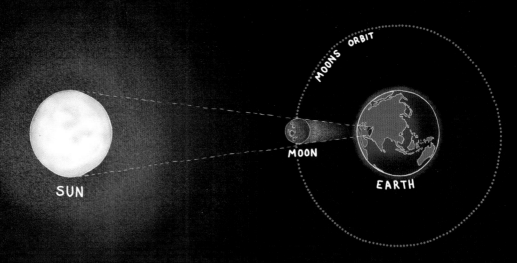